MW00916435

© 2021
Blake Karrington Presents

Who
CAN I
RUN TO

A Novel By

BLAKE KARRINGTON

AMANDA

"Aaron, I'm calling you again, leaving the fifth message. This shit is starting to get old. I know you see me calling. Can you just answer the phone or at least send me a text so that I know that you're good? .... I love you." Damn I sounded so pathetic. Like one of those women that I would talk cold shit about. Ughh, this bullshit was so unbecoming. Hanging up the phone, I tucked it back in my purse and rejoined Tracey and Eniko. We were having lunch at TGI Friday's, at Eniko's request of course.

"Everything alright boo?" Tracey asked as I sat down.

"Yeah, girl. I had to use the bathroom and got caught up on the phone with Aaron."

"Oh, okay, how is he doing?"

"You know Aaron always on the go. I couldn't even tell you how he was doing. His ass don't sit down long enough for me to even ask." I laughed lightly.

"I hear you. Well, I already paid the bill and I gotta drop Niko off to Micah at his office before I go to work." I was so proud of my cousin. She was a year clean and made a whole 180 . She was now working as a teacher's assistant and had finally gotten back to her life before the drugs. My girl had even been out on a few dates. What was more amazing was that in acknowledgement of her milestone, Micah offered to go back to court to put a joint custody agreement in place. And that was why he would always be Brother/Cousin-in-law in my eyes.

"Don't worry about Niko boo, I'll take her. I have to stop by there anyway to go over some things with Kelly regarding the shop." I saw my cousin's eyes turn up in her head and I smirked. She still wasn't a fan of Kelly, but they both remained civil for Niko's sake.

"Thank you Manda. Let me get going. Love you sweetie." She kissed Niko's cheek and was off. We waited for the waiter to wrap Niko's food up before leaving also.

I loved that my family was thriving. I wish I could say the same for myself. I mean, I was thriving in the workplace. I worked at a hair salon and had recently been taking steps to opening my own in the next few months. With Kelly and Domonique's help, I was able to find a rental space that would fit six booths comfortably as well as an area for therapeutic massage, should I choose to use that degree. While my career was coming along nicely, my relationship was the pits.

I couldn't even tell you where Aaron and I went wrong. We had been together since High school. He was truly the love of my life. Like Micah, he was a supplier. He dealt in pills though. Aaron was that nigga throughout High school and well into College. Of course, I was proud to be the lady on his arm. We'd traveled the world together, dined at the finest restaurants, and made nasty, bed breaking love in the most exquisite places. So, for us to be in the space we were now, had me questioning every-thing. As of late, he had been distant and very unaffectionate.

As I drove, I checked my phone every so often to see if he'd responded to any of my countless voicemails or text messages. Seeing that my phone was dry, I dropped it back in the cup holder. Aaron had been gone a full week and I hadn't spoken to him since he'd left our apartment. I didn't like to nag when he was away on business, but goddamn I was his woman, the least he could have done was checked in. Sometimes I felt like we were living two different lives. I looked like I had it altogether on the outside, but on the inside, I was crumbling.

Not having Tracey to worry about anymore was now forcing me to actually have to deal with my own problems head on. That was frightening to me; now having to face my own reality.

"Aunty Manda," Niko called out to me, interrupting my thoughts.

"Yes boo." I turned the radio down to give her my attention.

"Do you want kids someday?" Her question threw me off guard because even I hadn't thought about kids since the last conversation blow up I had with Aaron. During our High school days, we would always talk about having at least two kids, a boy for me and a little girl for him. He wanted our children to have a mixture of both of our personalities. Somewhere down the line that became a fantasy I only wanted for myself. Aaron made it clear that that was no longer in the cards for us.

"So, you sitting here today telling me you no longer want children?" I asked, completely baffled by what I was hearing coming out of Aaron's mouth.

"Yes, that's what I'm saying," he spoke nonchalantly. Picking up his fork he put a piece of the succulent stuffed chicken I had cooked perfectly for dinner and put it in his mouth. Here I was seated in my La Perla lingerie, all hot and ovulating for my man and he hit me with this bull.

I sat back in my seat with my arms crossed tightly across my chest. "Wow, and you say that shit like it's so simple."

"It is so simple Manda. I don't want kids."

"Well what the hell have we been planning for this whole time? I have a whole ovulation kit in our bathroom, down to the calendar hanging on the wall and notifications set on my phone and yours."

"Things change Amanda, people change."

"They sure the fuck do. I just wished you would have told me that. You could've kept me in the know about this sudden change after ten plus years." I pushed my food away from me and got up from the table.

That night I cried myself to sleep. Aaron came to console me and we had sex. To further insult me, he made sure to pull out. He was dead serious about the no kids thing. The next morning he was off again, and there was a gift on the table like nothing ever happened.

"Yeah, I want kids one day Niko. I'm hoping I can have a little person that's as dope as you." I squeezed her cheek and she giggled.

"I don't know aunty. I'm one of a kind, my dad says."

"He's right about that." I smiled. We pulled into the parking lot of E Luxe Realty and parked. Entering the office we were greeted by Tara who had the phone in the crook of her neck and seemed to be flustered. I asked if she was good and she gave me a thumbs up. "Hey, boo thang, what you up to?" I peeked into Kelly's office where she was seated in front of the computer.

"Hey girl and my little one." She hugged both Niko and I.

"Hey Kelly, is my daddy here?"

"Yeah, he's in there with your uncles. Go ahead and go right in."

"What about my brother?" She asked excitedly. Niko had taken to the big sister role like a fish in water.

"He's in there too. Ya daddy said they were having guy talk, but you know that means nothing to you." She winked and so did Niko. We knew for a fact that her dad would have a problem with anyone else interrupting him, but Niko, his princess, had full run of the castle. She ran off and I sat down across from Kelly.

"I guess it was 'bring your baby to the job' day, huh?"

"Girl, it's been like that everyday. It was the only way I was able to return to work. If it was up to Micah, I'd be home with MJ until he was six years old."

I chuckled because I saw first hand how bad Micah was with Niko when she was born. I knew he was a serious problem with his junior. "Oh, trust me girl, I know. That dude is a fool behind his kids."

"Chile, and to think I actually did that grapefruit trick thinking I was going to get my way and hire a nanny. Before I put that nigga to sleep, he made sure to tell me wasn't nobody gon' be watching his son, but me for at least the first six months."

"Bitch, not the grapefruit...and you still came out on the losing end?." Now, I was in a fit of laughter just imagining all that work for nothing.

"It ain't that funny," she laughed at herself. "What you doing here anyway, other than dropping Niko off?"

"I wanted to get your opinion on some ideas I saw online for the interior design of the shop."

"Oh, okay cool. I'm scheduled for a virtual meeting in an hour, so I have time. Let me see what you got." I pulled out my phone to show her some of my ideas that I had sketched and also some photos I saved from Pinterest. I could've sent these things via email, but I was avoiding going home to an empty place.

"These are really good Amanda. I really like the soft undertones that you're going with."

"Thank you boo. I can't wait to get in that place and make it one of a kind. I already started interviewing stylists. I even have two girls down at A Beautiful You, who want to be a part of the shop when I leave."

"That's wassup. Okay, my girl out there recruiting!"

"You know I'm on my job baby." I slapped fives with her.

"Hey babe, you busy?" I turned to find Micah entering with baby MJ in his hand and Kaiser and Karma behind him. I sucked my teeth seeing Kaiser lick his full lips at me. That man knew he was fine with his platinum fronts on the bottom of his teeth and his thick locs looking like he was a Chicago rapper.

"Not right now, wassup?"

"Ooh, gimmie my little man." I rubbed some of the hand sanitizer from Kelly's desk into my hands before reaching for MJ.

"Aye, Amanda," Kaiser called out to me, "I got a big man you can hold." He stuck out his tongue and humped the air.

"Kaiser, this office is PG-13 sir," Kelly let him know and Micah laughed, walking over to kiss her. They were so cute.

"There wasn't no PG-13 sounds coming out of this room when I got here a little while ago," he said, putting them on front street.

"Ooh, you get on my nerves," Kelly chuckled, throwing a box of tissues from her desk at him.

"Hey Karma, how you doing?" I spoke as Micah bent down to kiss my cheek.

"I'm good mama."

"Say, bruh, that's enough of the friendly shit. Don't be putting yo lips on my woman," Kaiser scolded his brother.

"She don't want yo ass fool."

"Exactly," I agreed.

"Yeah, whatever." Kaiser responded

I spent another few minutes fawning over the baby before Kelly kicked us all out to take her meeting. I said my goodbyes to Niko and the guys before making my way back out the building. I was off work today, so homebound it was for me.

"Ay, Manda, hold on real quick," I heard Kaiser call out to me. I stopped to see what he wanted. "Where you off to?"

"Home, nosey."

"Why I gotta be all that?"

"Is that what you stopped me for?"

"Why you gotta be so mean to a nigga? I stopped you

because I wanted to know if you wanted to go grab a quick bite to eat."

"I ate already," I answered quickly.

"Well shit, come watch me eat then. I really just want to be in your presence to be honest with you. You be igging a nigga hard."

I sucked my teeth and rolled my eyes. "That's because I have a man Kaiser and you know that."

"Who, that nigga Aaron?"

"Bye Kaiser," I went to walk away and he grabbed me by my arm lightly.

"Nah, forreal, you still fuck with dude?"

"Yes."

"Oh, well, I thought. You know what, never mind what I thought. Enjoy the rest of ya day ma." He turned and walked away before I could ask him to tell me what he thought. Shaking my head, I kept going to my car. Another weekend I'd be spending alone, yay me.

2

KAISER

"How'd it go lover boy? She shot you down again?" Karma clowned as I re entered Micah's office. "Nigga, shut up. Amanda still playing hard to get."

"You keep telling yourself that bro. I don't know how you play hard to get when you're already in a relationship. That's not called playing hard to get bro, that's called, already gotten." Both he and Micah got a good laugh at my expense. Even I had to chuckle a little. I had been after Amanda for years and she still wouldn't give a nigga no rap. Kept feeding me that, *I got a man,* bullshit. But I never seen them out anywhere together. If it wasn't for me halfway knowing the nigga from the streets, I wouldn't have even believed he existed. Whatever he and Amanda had going on ain't have shit to do with me. I just had to get her to understand that.

"Yo, Cah, let me get Manda number bro."

"Nah, I'm not giving you her number without her permission. You might fuck around and send her a pick of your johnson and have her man over there bugging out."

"And I'll beat his ass soon as I hear he tried to jump stupid.

9

Dick pics are so six months ago anyway. That shit played out now." He looked at me like I was crazy before busting out laughing.

"Karma get ya brother. This nigga is a nutcase, pause."

"Man, you owe me anyway for playing chauffeur for Kelly's birthday party and yo ass ain't paid up yet."

"Aight man, witcho cry baby ass. I'm not giving you her number though. I'ma leave my unlocked phone on my desk while I go to the bathroom." It didn't take long for me to catch on. I grabbed his phone as soon as he was out of the room and screenshot Amanda's number from his contacts.

"You wild for that bro."

"Whatever man, I'm out. I gotta go see a woman about a peach." I winked and he laughed waving me off. He knew that meant I was about to slide up in something wet. Just because I was vying for Amanda's attention didn't mean that I wasn't out here doing my own thing. Hopping in my X5, I drove over to my homegirl Ariane's house for a midday quicky. Ariane was a chick I'd met at Karma's club a while ago. She was cool peoples and for the most part she had her shit together.

Her only flaw was she acted as if she was on the same page with me when I told her that I wasn't looking for a relationship. Not only was I not looking for a relationship, but I was looking to chill with no strings attached. That meant, I wasn't taking you on no dates, I don't want no parts in yo' social media and when you see me in the street you get the universal head nod. I laid everything out once I started fucking with a female that way she could make the decision on whether or not she wanted to be around me. Most of them did, and who was I to deny them?

Ariane lived Uptown in the projects and being the loose cannon I was, I kept two bangers on me at all times. These little niggas out here was living reckless and trying to make a name for themselves by any means. A nigga had one time to get outta pocket with me and I was turning this bitch into the Wild Wild

West on my own. If I got my niggas involved it was sure to look like Independence Day. I parked in the parking lot right underneath her window, so that I had a direct view of my car.

Getting out, I pulled up my pants and made sure my banger was secure. People knew me everywhere, just like they knew Karma and Micah. But they more so stayed out of the way since Micah had the realty company and Karma the club. I was usually the one in the streets making plays. This was one project building that we allowed some low level niggas to get money, but they made sure they paid their taxes and all was right with the world.

"What's good Kaiser?" One of the dudes standing on one of the park benches spoke my name like we knew each other. Not wanting to crush his ego, I gave him a head nod. I hated when grown men spoke to other grown men like they were familiar with them, knowing damn well they didn't know them from a can of paint. That shit irritated me. Keeping it moving, I took the stairs instead of fucking with the death trap of an elevator they had. The last time I pulled up on Ariane it took me twenty minutes just to get to the fourth floor where she lived.

Jogging up the steps, I was glad that the hallway door was already open because there was no way I was touching that shit with my hands. Niggas was living real foul in this building. Before I could knock on her door, I could hear music blasting from her apartment. Shorty had to have been having a party to have her shit that loud. I didn't even bother knocking, I just shot her a text, letting her know I was at the door. Immediately, the volume went from a fifty to a cool fifteen. I heard locks turning and she opened the door wearing a robe and a towel was tied tightly on her head.

"Hey Kaiser."

"Wassup ma, what you got going on?"

"Nothing, just getting out the shower. ome in." I stepped inside and it was like entering another world. Quite different from the littered hallways. Ariane's apartment was clean, she didn't have too much in it though. "You can head on back to my room. I'm gonna change real quick."

I didn't know what the point of her changing was when the objective was to get naked anyway. I went back into her room and waited on her. The flat screen tv on the wall was playing an episode of Martin, so I was able to entertain myself while I waited. By the time she came inside, she was dressed in a short tank top and a thong. Her ass was looking juicy too. She sat down on the edge of her bed and stared at me.

"What we doing here ma?" I asked wondering why she wasn't ass naked with her ass up in the air.

"I thought we could talk for a little bit."

"We did talk...over text when we agreed to link."

"Dang Kaiser, you can't hold a conversation with me now?" She turned her lip up with an attitude.

"You losing me Ariane. I came over here to get some pussy. You wanna talk about your feelings and clearly somewhere in the text we missed the others intentions." I got up, ready to head out because I wasn't beat for this shit today.

"Is pussy really all you think about?"

"Nah, money too and what I'm gonna eat in the next few hours."

"Whatever Kaiser, come on and lets just get it over with." She went to lift her shirt over her head and I stopped her.

"Nah, I'm good. If you're not about to give it to me willingly, I'm not about to feel like I'm forcing you. I'll hit you some other time, when we both on the same page." I may have been a lot of things, but one thing I wasn't was a thirsty nigga.

I NEEDED MY DREADS RETWISTED, so I planned to use that as a reason to hit Amanda's phone. Getting out of bed, I prayed for

God to cover me before going to handle my hygiene. During my shower, I thought back to the first day I was introduced to Amanda. It wasn't the best introduction either. I walked in on her crying in the bathroom at one of Micah's game nights.

"*Oh, damn, I'm sorry ma. I should've knocked.*"

"*Yes, you should've,*" she snapped on me while dabbing at her eyes.

"*You good?*"

"*Yes, I am and I'm also still occupying this bathroom, so could you get out?*"

"*Damn, you mean. I'ma close the door though because I gotta piss, but I'm coming back and I wanna know why you in here crying.*" I closed the door and once I was done getting myself together, I went back to the bathroom to find her, but it was empty. Heading back into the game room, I spotted her in the corner, trying to look as if nothing was wrong.

"*You ready to tell me what happened?*" She looked up at me and rolled her eyes.

"*No, I'm not.*"

"*Unfortunately for you, you don't have a choice. I plan to stalk you the whole night until you tell me. The name's Kaiser by the way.*" I sat down next to her without an invite and for an hour we sat in silence watching everyone else interact with each other. She could've gotten up at any time, but she didn't.

"*I had an argument with my boyfriend. Can you leave me alone now?*"

"*What y'all argue about?*"

"*Now, that's really none of your business.*"

"*Aight, well, you too pretty to be crying no name.*"

"*No name?*"

"*Yeah, I gave you my name, but you haven't told me yours, so no name it is.*"

"*My name is Amanda.*"

"*Nice to meet you Amanda.*" I stood to leave. "*Word to the wise Amanda, any man that makes you cry any tears other than tears of joy, is not the man for you."*

For the remainder of the night I watched her from afar as she tried to enjoy herself, but nothing seemed to work. Eventually she left and I got a quick rundown on her from Micah. I would run into her a few more times, but she had no rap for me. I was still intrigued by her and wanted to see wassup. A nigga was getting older and I didn't want to be one of them old dudes with young kids who totally couldn't relate. I needed to find me a good woman like Micah had done. Once I was fully dressed, I sent a text to Amanda's phone.

Me: Good morning beautiful.

Manda: Who is this?

Me: It's Kaiser, yo future baby daddy.

Manda: How'd you get my number?

Me: That's not important. I need my dreads retwisted. You think you can help me out?

Manda: Sorry, no can do, I have a busy day.

Me: I got a band for you.

Manda: I'll see you when you get here.

I laughed at her quick response once I offered that thousand dollars. To tell you the truth Amanda could get anything she wanted out of me. After putting her money together, I gathered my hair products and headed to the salon she worked at. As soon as I entered the place, all eyes were on me. The groupies spoke, while the women that may not have known me looked like they were trying to figure out a way to get to know me.

"Man, come sit down and let me do yo head," Manda called out, having had enough of me already and I hadn't even sat in her chair yet.

"Well, hello to you too mean ass."

"Hi, Kaiser. Are these the products you want me to use?" She said referring to the bag I held in my hand.

"Yeah, it's all Taliah Waajid products."

14

"Alright, did you wash your hair yet?"

"Nah," I lied. "I'm paying you a stack. I need you to do all that." I wanted to spend as much time with her as possible. Plus, I wanted to watch them titties jiggle as she washed my hair. She sucked her teeth and walked me over to the wash bowl.

"You have quite the audience," she commented while lathering my hair with shampoo. I felt a little heat coming up off of her. My baby was jealous. I liked that shit. She needed to know that she had nothing to worry about.

"Yeah, they have their eyes on me while I have mine on you." She looked down and my eyes bore into hers. Unable to hold my stare, she turned away. I was wearing Amanda down and she was powerless to stop it.

3

AMANDA

Being around Kaiser's ignorant ass always gave me unwanted butterflies. He made me smile when I didn't want to and laugh even when shit wasn't funny. It was something about his aura that was inviting, yet there were warning signs that came along with it. While in my own head, I glanced down and his eyes were zoomed in on my cleavage.

"So, you just gonna look right at my titties?"

He smirked cockily. "Shit, they're looking at me." I rolled my eyes and continued washing his hair. There was no point in trying to reprimand him. After giving his hair a good washing, I wrapped a towel around his head and he followed me to my station.

"You have any idea of what you want done?" I asked while towel drying his hair. I loved the blonde and black dreads he had. I had an idea of what I wanted to do, but wanted him to think he had a choice.

"Do whatever ma. I need to be outta here by one though," he said while in his phone. Being the nosey person I am, I couldn't help but to lean over his shoulder and snoop. Seeing a picture of a naked girl on the screen with the text, *I'm horny* attached to it, I was disgusted.

"Low budget ass hoes," I whispered under my breath while shaking my head.

"Until you give a nigga a chance, this is what I gotta deal with." I guess I wasn't whispering after all.

"Kaiser please. If that's what you fucking with now, then you'll never have a chance with me."

"Oh, so I have a chance right now?"

I put my own damn foot in my mouth with that statement. "No, that's not what I said. And I have a man, you know that." He smirked and put his eyes back on his phone. Why is it that every man that tried to pursue me had that same reaction when I mentioned being in a relationship? It's like they knew something I didn't.

For the remaining two hours, I retwisted his dreads with no words spoken between us. Just light stares here and there. I counted at least four of the six stylists that came over to my station asking for stuff. While I was annoyed at the, *"Can I use your hair rollers?"* and other frivolous questions, Kaiser was getting a kick out of it. They were just thirsty as fuck. I was glad to get him up and out when he came from under the dryer.

"That's what I'm talking about bae. You got ya man out here looking good." He checked himself out in the mirror, licking his lips and rubbing his hands together.

"You aight." I downplayed it when in my head I was praising his good looks.

"Can I give you your money over dinner tonight?" He asked, turning to face me.

"Nah, I'll take my cash now, thank you." I held my hand out for him to grease my palm. Reaching into his pocket, he pulled out a knot and peeled off ten one hundred dollar bills.

"We'll talk about dinner at a later date then." He placed the money in my shirt and kissed my cheek. I wiped it off quickly and he laughed. "I'll see you later bae." He waved bye to his fan club as he exited.

"Mmmm, that man know he fine as fuck," Denise, the owner of the salon spoke while fanning herself. She was always lusting over any man that walked through the doors. If I didn't know her I would think she wasn't getting any at home, but I did and Denise was getting plenty. Just not from her own man. For that, we didn't get along on a personal level, but there was a mutual respect regarding business.

"Girl, ain't he though. Got a bitch all moist and shit," Diamond, another stylist and Denise's sister chimed in. "Is he single Amanda? Shit, it don't even matter, hook a sister up." Like her sister, Diamond was a bed hopper as well. It was a good thing that I wasn't feeling Kaiser because if I was, they would surely have me in my feelings.

"I'm not sure if he's single or not, but if he is I don't think you're his type," I said shutting her down.

"And what's that supposed to mean?" She asked, offended.

"It means what I said, I know Kaiser and you're not his type." She was most definitely his type. Kaiser liked hoes, but he wasn't gonna be fucking on this one, especially when I had to work with her. Again, this has nothing to do with me wanting him or anything like that.

Her hand went to her hip and she snaked her neck as she spoke, "Oh, so you his type? I swear you think you better than everybody up in here." Diamond was known for starting confrontation with the stylist because she felt like she could, being that she was Denise's sister. The other stylists let her talk shit to them in fear of losing their spots at one of the premiere beauty shops in the city. I, on the other hand, didn't give a damn if she was kin to the president. Wasn't no bitch gon' come for me.

"I don't think I'm better than anyone. And let me be the first to tell you, I'm everybody's type. Please watch how you address me."

She went to say something else, but Denise called her. It was a good thing she did too because with the mouth I had on me, I had the ability to cut yo ass deep. Then she was gonna wanna fight and lets just say, her sister spared her the embarrassment. While waiting for my next client, I checked my phone to see if I had any missed calls or messages from Aaron. Seeing that my phone was dry, I texted him again. Now, I was pissed off.

Me: At this point, I feel like I'm stalking my own damn man. You don't have to worry about hearing from me after this and don't even think about bringing yo ass home.

I put my head down and counted to ten. I wanted so bad to break down and cry, but I wouldn't give these women the satisfaction. A deep breath and a quick reminder to myself that I was that bitch and wasn't no better bitch breathing, put me in a better headspace. My phone vibrated, and it was my client letting me know she was looking for a parking space and would be in shortly. I took the time to go to the bathroom. Walking back out, Domonique was sitting at my station.

"Hey boo, how'd you make out with parking?" I asked, giving her a quick hug.

"Heyy, I found a spot around the corner. Girl, yo little receptionist got a nasty ass attitude." We didn't have one set receptionist and when I looked over at the front desk, Diamond was sitting behind it.

"Oh, girl she ain't no receptionist. She probably salty from how I hurt her feelings earlier."

"Hmph, she was about to get chin checked, but I kept it cute because I don't want you out here looking crazy." I laughed at Domonique's spunk.

"Trust me, she don't want no problems. What's been going on?" I pulled out the braiding hair that I had set aside for her and got it set up.

"Girl, nothing much, just came from a showing. I'm so happy you had an opening today because this rat nest on my head got me looking less than presentable out in these streets." I laughed at her dramatics. Domonique had a head full of curly hair slicked up nicely in a puff ball. Taking it out of the ponytail, there was nothing nappy about it.

"Get that money boo. And this hair is beautiful, you playing. It smell good too. Now, remember, I told you these knotless braids are gonna take about five to six hours being that you want them long."

"I got my iPad and I know you can hold a conversation. Let's do this boo." I got the hair prepped and went to work. Hair was my passion. I'd been braiding since I was younger. When my mother caught on to how talented I was, she began teaching me how to perfect my skills. I could do any style of braids and with completing cosmetology school, I was now well rounded.

As I worked on Domonique's hair, I found myself thinking about Kaiser. No matter how many times I turned him down, he still showed interest in me. He didn't care about my relationship with Aaron and made sure to let me know whenever we were in each others presence. Ughh, I can't believe I was sitting here allowing this man to consume my thoughts.

"Amanda, girl did you hear what I said?" Domonique stared at me through the mirror.

"I'm sorry boo, I zoned out for a minute. What did you say?"

"I asked if you had any plans tonight? Me and Kelly were going to stop by Karma's later for a drink." I wanted to say no, but with Aaron ignoring my calls I knew he wouldn't be home tonight, so what the hell.

"I could use a drink."

"It's on then. Bring out yo' best shit cause we about to tear the club up." We high fived each other and I continued braiding. I was turning up tonight, Aaron who?

"WELL, alright bitch. You not playing with em' tonight," Domonique gassed my head up and I took it all in. I did a little twirl in my jumpsuit, that fit my body just right. The black cat suit I had on had mesh material from the waist up, showing the silhouette of my perky D cup breasts. It hung off my shoulders, and the butterfly tattoos I had along my shoulder blade were on display. Standing at five foot six with no shoes on, in heels I looked like a stallion.

I did a light beat on my round face. Unlike the other girls I didn't need any extra eye lashes. My mother had blessed me with a long set that only needed a little eye liner. People often compared me to Kelly Rowland and I took it as the highest compliment. She was my favorite out of the whole Destiny's Child crew. The only difference between the two of us was that I was a little thicker and I loved every curvy inch of me.

"Yes boo, you look da fuck good," Kelly added from the passenger side. "Hurry up and get in before Micah ring my phone tryna renig on being home with the baby tonight." I laughed at Kelly because Micah was such a hater. It still amazed me how cool Kelly and I had become since I'd met her. If I could have hand picked anyone to be with Micah outside of Tracey then Kelly was it. She loved Eniko like her own and she did her best to avoid any possible confrontation with Tracey.

"I'm ready to get so drunk that I don't even remember my name in the morning." Getting in the backseat, Domonique passed back my own bottle of Veuve Clicquot Rich Rose.

"Start now sis. Kelly is the designated driver for the night since she's breastfeeding." Kelly's head snapped in her direction. "What? Those were your words, not mine," she said with a smile.

"Girl, this big ass bottle coming right inside the club with me too," I said while rolling down the window to pop it open.

"I changed my mind. I'm drinking too shit. At least a two cup minimum. I'll pump and dump when I get home." I was with her, shit turn up, she needed the break. If she thought that was gonna fly, she had another thing coming. I sipped on the Hennessy and moved my body to the music that played throughout the car. I hoped that I didn't get in this lounge and get the crying about Aaron. Liquor always made me emotional and sometimes irate.

Karma's was packed out on this Saturday night. We breezed pass the line that wrapped around the corner and went right inside. Immediately, my hands went in the air when I heard Faith Evans, *Love like this* play throughout the club. The song was a classic and you couldn't help but to tear the floor up when it came on. I danced through the sea of people and followed Kelly and Domonique to V.I.P. As the bouncer opened the door, my two step came to a holt seeing a female descending the steps with Kaiser behind her.

"Wassup Kaiser," Kelly spoke and so did Domonique. He gave them both hugs while the girl stood off to the side.

"What's good y'all? Hey bae," he said to me. The ladies, including no name looked in my direction to see my response.

"I just saw you earlier," I said smartly.

"And look what god did. He made it so that I was able to see your beautiful face again. Y'all go on up and get comfortable. I'll have a couple bottles sent up to the table. Karma and Cah are up there already." Kelly nearly ran upstairs before either of us could say a word. I rolled my eyes at Kaiser and kept it moving.

"I thought you were on baby duty tonight," I said to Micah, giving him half a hug.

"I am, this one of my babies right here." He motioned to Kelly and pulled her into his arms. He kissed her like he hadn't been with her a little while ago.

"Eww, don't make me barf," Domonique teased, making us laugh. "C'mon Amanda, I came to get drunk not watch them make love in the club." Kelly stuck her tongue out at us while we walked away. It didn't take long before I put Aaron to the back of my mind and spent time getting fucked up with Domonique. We danced to every song that played. Whoever they had DJ'ing was doing the damn thing.

"Get that shit D," I hyped Domonique up as she dropped to the floor and twerked. Her booty bounced like two basketballs. She had me ready to throw some dollars, sis was tearing the floor up. She smiled and stuck her tongue out. I couldn't help but to put my hands on my knees and join her. Feeling hands up against my waist, I turned to find none other than Kaiser trying to catch what I was throwing.

Feeling good from the drinks, I just kept on moving. By the time I finished throwing my ass in a circle, I felt his hard on against my ass and the dj had slowed it down. Trey Songz, *Panty Droppa* played and I sensually grinded on Kaiser's hard on. I knew it shocked him because I was shocking the shit out of myself. I closed my eyes and it felt like just he and I were in the room.

"We been spending time, wanna make ya mine. When you're not around, you're still on my mind," Kaiser sang into my ear and my eyes shot open. This negro could sing. He went to wrap his arms around me and before I could melt, a female could be heard shouting his name.

"Kaiser!" We both turned and the girl from the steps stormed towards us. "You a little too close aren't you?" She questioned Kaiser who seemed more concerned with the fact that I had stopped moving. I snickered and moved out of his embrace. "I don't see what's so fucking funny."

I sobered up real quick, now realizing the animosity was toward me. "This ain't what you want boo. You betta direct that energy that way." I pointed to Kaiser and went to walk away again. For the second time I was avoiding confrontation, but I guess she had something to prove.

"This energy is for the both of y'all."

"Aye, chill with that shit. All that ain't even necessary," Kaiser jumped in. He looked at me and I rolled my eyes in annoyance before walking off. Yet another reason to add to my list as to why I wouldn't give him the time of day if I wasn't taken.

4

DOMONIQUE

I looked on at the exchange between Amanda, Kaiser and the unknown female we saw him with earlier and shook my head. Any person with eyes could see that Kaiser was gone over Amanda, including her. I thought for sure that she was going to swing on the unknown, but she played it cool. I liked that. My motto was to never let a bitch see you sweat, under no circumstances.

I downed the last of my Dusse and apple juice and sat it on the table. I was all danced out and had reached my drink limit. Before I could try to suppress it, a yawn escaped my mouth. Yeah, it was time for me to take it in. Standing up, I went to let Kelly and Amanda know that I was ready to go. Making my way over to them, where they stood with Micah, Karma blocked my path.

"Leaving so soon?" He asked. I could smell his minty breath, mixed with some kind of exotic weed.

"I am if you let me pass."

"I'll let you pass if you let me take you home." My lip curled up and I took a step back.

"Now, why would I let you do that when I'm very capable of doing so myself?" I asked folding my arms across my chest.

"You've been knocking drinks back all night ma. I'm just trying to be helpful."

"Usually people are that way when they're asked for help. Thanks, but no thanks." I moved around him and made it to the ladies who were now talking amongst themselves. "Hey y'all I'm bout ready to take it in for the night."

"Me too girl. My night was going good up until now."

"Yeah, I saw ya boo's boo was making a scene."

"Oh, you got jokes huh?" She said catching on to the fact that I referred to Kaiser as her boo. Kelly and I laughed.

"I was just saying the same thing, D. She know Kaiser got a thing for her," Kelly added.

"Anyway, I'm ready whenever you are. And I just might be a little more sober than you so I can drive if you don't mind handing over your keys." I was with Amanda's suggestion, but didn't get to respond before Kaiser came out of nowhere to speak for me.

"That won't be necessary because I'm taking her home and you," he pointed to me, "will be chauffeured by Karma."

"Uh, wrong. How you gonna tell me whose driving in my car?"

"Exactly, and I'm not going anywhere with you. You better go find that Erica Mena knock off and take her wack ass home," Amanda spoke with a lot of animosity.

"You do know she has a man at home right Kaiser," Kelly spoke my thoughts.

"And you do know that I didn't give a fuck when I first met her and give a fuck less now, right. Now that we got that out the way, we out. Get home safe y'all." He grabbed Amanda's hand and gave her the face that dared her to pull away. To my surprise, she complied and walked off with him.

"Girl, he gon' get Amanda ass, mark my words." I nodded

my head in agreement.

"Well, alright I guess I'm riding solo. I'll see you at the office on Monday boo." I kissed Kelly's cheek and made my way downstairs to the exit. When I got to my car, Karma stood up against the passenger side door on his phone. "Umm, is there a reason why you're standing at my truck?"

He lifted his head and gave a sheepish smile. "I'm here to make sure you get home safe. You look like you have it together, but like I said before, you knocked back a couple drinks back there. I'd feel better escorting you home."

"I thought I told you that I didn't need any help. I'm a big girl baby, I got me." I went to walk to the driver's side and he put his hand on my waist to stop me.

"Don't fight me on this beautiful. Trust me, you won't win. Keys please, or I can hot wire your shit, your choice." He held his hand out and I was turned on by his dominance. I wouldn't let his cocky ass know that.

"You're not getting my keys, Karma. That tough shit may work on the chicks you associate yourself with, but it won't work with me."

"No problem, I'm sure my skills are still up to par." He put his phone away and tried to walk around to my driver's side.

"Wait," I yelled out to stop him, "You're really serious huh?" The look on his face said he was deadass. I handed over my keys and proceeded to get in on the passenger side. He unlocked it and I climbed in. I rattled off my address and leaned back in my seat. "Now, remember this is not your car. Drive my baby like you have some sense, please and thank you."

"Aight, beautiful," was his response. I closed my eyes and went along for the ride. Karma was not about to suck me in with that smooth shit. I didn't even want to be alone in the car with him, but his threats to hot wire my car made the decision easy for me.

"You got a man at home that I need to know about?"

I opened my eyes and glanced over at him. "Now you wanna be concerned?"

"Concerned for me, no, but for him, yes."

"So, you just gon' low key threaten my man?' I was both shocked and still turned on.

"I don't make threats and you already answered my question for me. If you had a man you would've came right out and said that."

"You're right. I don't have a man and I'm not looking for one either." I hoped he caught onto what I was saying. Karma was easy on the eyes. Hell, he was fine as fuck, but he needed not to waste his time trying to holla. He didn't respond and I was okay with that. It was another 45 minutes before we made it to my apartment building in lower Manhattan.

"You got a parking spot?" He asked as I picked up my purse.

"Yeah, in the parking garage, but you can park it on the street for now." We found a spot across from the building and got out. It was going on two in the morning and the time was starting to catch up to me.

"Here's your keys." He handed me my key fob.

"Thanks. How are you getting home?" I questioned.

"Don't worry about me beautiful, I'll manage. You just make sure to let someone know that you got upstairs safely."

"Will do. Thanks for the ride and goodnight Karma."

"Anytime." Just as I went to walk off, a black Audi pulled up and he got in on the passenger side. The car didn't pull off until I made it inside the building. Karma had proven himself to be a gentleman, that's for sure. I rode the elevator upstairs to my place and a somber feeling came over me. Sticking my key inside the door, the fresh scent of flowers hit my nostrils. Flowers were my thing; evidently being lonely was too.

To the outside world, I was Domonique Sawyer, the real estate beast and the poster girl for independent women. You know that Neyo song, "Shawty Got Her Own"? He made that song about me. And I'd been getting it on my own since I was fifteen. My mother died suddenly from a brain aneurysm I knew nothing about. She was my best friend and I was devastated when I lost her. From there I was shuffled between my aunt and grandmother's house. That lasted until what money she left over dried up and that's when the fake love stopped.

They shunned me and my last stop was my god mother, Viv's house. She was my mother's best friend and far from the nurturing type. Viv liked to drink, cuss, fuss, and above all else she liked to party. I never understood how she was best friends with my mother since they were polar opposites. I made sure I got to school everyday and had everything I needed.

Viv basically gave me a place to stay as long as I helped her with her hustling schemes. When I turned 18, I was over with her sending me to meet random men and luring them to places, *"If you ain't helping bring no money in here, you gots to get the fuck out on your own."* That was her speech as if I wasn't doing that already. Lucky for me and my book smarts, I was able to get a full scholarship to NYU that included room and board. My savings account sat nicely as well, thanks to my money management skills.

I graduated college with a degree in business management and a masters in hustling. The real estate thing just came natural for me. On top of being book and street smart, I was beautiful and my heart was pure. I bore a striking resemblance to my mother, with people often referring to me as her twin. We both had honey colored skin and big round, brown eyes.

My physique was that of a runners with a flat stomach, firm thighs and toned arms. The ass was very much fat and I had ample titties. Yea, I was that girl. Along with that, I had a knack for beautiful things and the gift of gab. Still, with all of this talent, my bomb looks and my great personality, I came home to an empty bed every night. Yeah, I know I told Karma that I wasn't looking for a man but that was the truth.

I wasn't looking, but it would be nice to have one. I was one of the very few women who didn't need a dude to buy me things. I could do that myself. I wanted someone who matched my ambition and drive. A friend before a lover. He needed to be able to make love to me mentally before he could stroke me physically.

Karma was damn fine. His six foot two inch thin, muscular frame with six-pack abs made him appear more mature than his actual age. His locs was full and pulled back tight hugging his scalp. Anyway, he was cool and I liked the way he carried himself when it came to his business. The thing that turned me off was the females that sure flocked to him. He was a true hoe magnet, but that usually came with a dude that had money. I was certainly not interested in being a part of the stable he had.

I took my shoes off at the door and set them on the shoe rack. Stepping into my Ugg slides, I made my way to my bedroom. Living alone was cool until night fell. I stripped out of my clothes and headed straight for the shower to wash off the club. After a twenty minute shower, I sent a group text to Kelly and Domonique letting them know that I made it home safe. It didn't take long after my head hit my Puffy Lux mattress before I was out like a light.

"So how'd the drop off go?" Kelly asked via FaceTime while I did my morning skincare routine.

"Gimmie a second. I didn't forget that I needed to curse you out. I thought I'd wait until later on in the day." I dried my face and looked into the camera to find Kelly snickering with her baby boy in her arms. "I'm not laughing heffa. You thought you was so slick. Do you know that man threatened to hot wire my damn car?"

She was laughing hard now with her hand over her mouth.

"Ooh, no he didn't."

"Yes, girl. I handed over my keys because you know I couldn't risk something happening to my baby." I spoke of my G-Wagon like it was a real person.

"My bad, my bad. He was watching you all night and when you got ready to leave he all but told me and Micah that he was taking you home." I shook my head at Karma's boldness.

"Lemme see lil man. I see his head over there wobbling, he hear my voice." She turned MJ around and his eyes lit up seeing me. For a few seconds we engaged in baby talk until Micah's hating self came over and snatched him up. "You're a hater," I yelled out to his back as he walked out the door.

"What you doing today?"

"It's Sunday, I'm just gonna chill in the house, get some work done, and binge watch The Wire." Sunday's were calm for me. I didn't do too much moving around and whatever I needed was already available in my house.

"Well alright girl, I was just checking on you. I'll see you tomorrow at the office."

"You think you slick heaux. You tryna rush me off the phone so you can go get some dick."

"And that's my business," she imitated Tabitha Brown's voice making me crack up laughing.

"Bye girl." Hanging up, I put my phone on vibrate and set it on the charger. Heading to the kitchen, I took out the ingredients to make myself some french toast and turkey sausage. As I set everything up on the kitchen counter, my doorbell rang. It was nine in the morning and I didn't have visitors unless it was Kelly. I probably should've threw a robe over my sports bra and boxer briefs, but what the hell, this is my house.

"Just a minute," I called out.

"Hurry up beautiful," I heard as I got closer. I froze, knowing the voice belonged to Karma. What the hell was this man doing at my door?

5

KARMA

I stood outside of Dominique's door with no real reason as to why I was there. After dropping her off a couple hours ago, I headed back to the club and stayed until closing. It had been my routine since I opened. I hadn't gotten around to hiring a full time general manager, so it was my job in the meantime. By the time I made it home, it was going on five in the morning. I slept for all of three hours before I was up again.

With Domonique fresh on my mind, I found myself in my car and headed to her place. I planned to tell her that I was in the neighborhood, so that she didn't think I was on some stalker shit. Being the patient man I am, I didn't bother knocking on the door a second time. Hearing the locks turn, the door opened and she stood on the other side of it in a robe and a scarf on her head.

"Really, Karma. What are you doing at my house? And don't try to hit me with that you were in the neighborhood line either."

"I wanted to see you again," I admitted. Her once stoned face relaxed a little but her shoulders were still tight. I was very observant so I knew that she still wasn't feeling me popping up.

"Okay," she folded her arms across her chest, "you seen me,

I'm good. You can go now." She snapped back into her feisty self just that quick.

"Damn, it's like that?"

"Yes. You can't just pop up unannounced and expect to be invited in with open arms. We are not like that Karma." Her face tightened and I smiled.

"You got that beautiful. My apologies, I'ma go." She didn't let me step back from the door good enough before she closed it. I shook my head and got back on the elevator to my car. Domonique had proven herself to be a brick wall that was gonna be hard to penetrate. She came off standoffish and it let me know that she was guarded.

I'd been watching her for a while since she'd started at the E Luxe. While a social butterfly, I'd never seen her with a dude. She was intriguing to say the least. Today's approach may not have been the best, but I'd be seeing her soon enough. Jumping in my car, I headed back to the crib to get some real sleep. Entering my building, I gave my door man a head nod and walked to the elevator. On the ride up, I thought about everything I wanted to get accomplished for the day.

I made use of my twenty four hours everyday. There were no do overs for me. I always made sure to use my time wisely. With me taking a step back from the streets, I put my all into my club. Karmas was the best business decision Micah could've ever encouraged me to make. Although I was no longer apart of the day to day activities of the streets like my brother, niggas still knew my body and I was only a phone call away.

Opening the door to my apartment, I heard noise coming from the kitchen. Pulling my blade from my pants pocket, I walked in that direction. If a motherfucka was able to bypass security and get into this overpriced ass building, they were gonna have hell to pay. Rounding the corner, my ex, Jerricka stood at my stove naked as the day she was born. It looked like she was trying to figure out how to use it.

Normally the sight of her round ass would've had me excited, but the last time we saw each other, I specifically told her to leave my key. So, I was less than enthused about her being up in my shit like it was cool. I tapped her on the shoulder and she jumped, pulling her headphones from her ears.

"Shit, you scared me Karma." She held her hand up to her chest and held her hand out like she was trying to catch her breath.

"Yo' ass wouldn't be scared if you wasn't in my shit." Looking around her, I noticed the breakfast items she had lined up on the counter. "And you about to burn my place down? You know yo ass can't cook."

"I'm just tryna do something nice for you Karma. I know the last time I was here, things got heated between us. I'm sorry for how I came off." I ignored her. Jerricka did this shit all the time to get her way.

"Go get ya clothes on Jerricka, and I'm not gonna repeat myself."

"But Karma…" she whined and I cut her off.

"Jerricka," I said her name again and gave her a look that let her know I wasn't playing. She caught my drift, and kept it moving. This was one of the benefits of growing up with a Muslim father. I knew how to abstain from women and food since we were forced to practice Ramadan every year. I know for a normal nigga the sight of some ass and food would have drove them crazy.

I put the pancake mix, eggs, and bacon back in the fridge. I can't believe this chick was really trying to kill me. Jerricka could barely boil an egg and here she was trying to make pancakes. We were in a relationship for eight months before I realized that being committed to one woman wasn't for me. I wasn't used to answering to anyone, so I cut her off with no love lost on my end. I also made sure that she wasn't confused as to why I broke it off either.

"I didn't come here to beef with you Karma. I really wanted to talk." She was now fully dressed in a pair of skin tight jeans, heels and one of my t-shirts.

"Bruh, how you…never mind. If you wanted to talk that's why they invented phones. You could've called me." I imagined that this was the same way Domonique felt when I pulled up on her. The difference here was, Jerricka was actually in my crib. "And why you still got a key to my crib?"

"I made an emergency copy. You know, in case of an emergency."

"The emergency is gonna be you in an ambulance if you don't give me my key and any other copy you may have," I threatened. I watched as she went into her purse and quickly produced my keys. "Thank you. Now it's time for you to step."

"Once I leave, I'm not coming back Karma. You not gonna just cut me off and then call me when you feel like it."

"I didn't call yo' ass here today Jerricka. Trust me, it's a wrap after the shit you pulled. You lucky I didn't poke yo ass up when I got in here. Go head man." I waved her off and she sucked her teeth while making her exit. Locking the door behind her, I crashed right on the couch.

"Look at this nigga, sleeping like a newborn baby." I opened my eyes to see my brother and Micah sitting across from me. Sitting up, I stretched and cracked my neck.

"I don't know what the fuck is going on today, but mother-fuckas need to stop thinking its cool to come up in my spot without calling to see if I'm in the mood for company."

Micah chuckled and Kaiser scoffed. "Nigga, I got a key."

"Yeah, for you to use in case of an emergency bro."

"Man whatever. I'll use it whenever I damn well please."

"And your ass will be keyless right along with Jerricka."

"Nigga—,"

"Y'all know y'all sound like two bitches right." As always Micah stepped in between one of me and Kaiser's many arguments. "Y'all ain't gon' never grow out of that shit." That statement was true.

"Man, what y'all doing here anyway?"

"Oh, now you wanna know," Kaiser patronized me.

"Shut the fuck up Kaiser, damn."

"Chill," Micah said, "we're here because I need to make a business trip." I knew what he meant by business. It was time to re up. "I figured you could use the vacation. You know, with you working so hard down at the club."

"Hell yeah. When we heading out there?"

"In two weeks. I'm taking Kelly too. She's never been out of the country and her mom agreed to watch MJ. Eniko will be with Tracey for the week."

"Aight, that gives me enough time to find a general manager to look after the club while I'm gone."

"And find somebody to bring witchu. I'm bringing Amanda and three's a crowd my nigga," Kaiser added.

"Amanda know you bringing her?" Micah asked what I was thinking, making me laugh.

"She will once Kelly invites her. I got this," he assured. This nigga didn't give up easily, I had to give him that.

"So, let me guess, you bringing Domonique?" Micah asked me.

"Nah, she ain't feeling the kid. I may get lucky though, if Kelly mentions it to her. If she do, I'm in there. Shawty bad, but mean as hell. That don't stop me from wanting to get to know her though."

"Well, you got two weeks to do that bro." Micah stood and held his hand out to dap me up. "I'ma get outta here. Today is family day." Giving him a manly hug, I walked him to the door while Kaiser remained seated.

"You ain't got nowhere to be?" I asked, closing the door behind Micah and returning back to my spot on the couch.

"Nah, today is family day for me too," he smirked. I laughed and threw a pillow at him.

"You a clown dawg." For the rest of the day, we ate, chilled and got high. Me and bro rarely had time to hang since we were always busy. I didn't take these moments for granted, especially after the passing of our pops, Koran. I missed my old man. He always told us the importance of sticking together. Our dad was our hero. "Aye Kai, you ever think about pops?"

"All the time," he answered back, his eyes halfway opened. The high had set in.

"Me too man. What you think he'd say if he seen us now?"

"Man, y'all lil niggas is some male hoes." We both cracked up laughing. "That nigga would've been clowning us."

"Yeah, and mama just wasn't shit," he spat. I left that conversation alone. Our mother was a sensitive topic. According to my pops, she had made it clear that she didn't want to be a mother. He, on the other hand, wanted kids, so he basically trapped her. She was in the wind not too long after giving birth to us. Leaving my father to raise us alone. The only time she really reached out was when she wanted or needed something. I had a soft heart for her but Kaiser for some reason acted like he didn't care. I knew deep down inside he yearned for that motherly love just like myself. But his ass would never admit it.

"I'ma settle down soon," I announced making Kaiser sit up from the position where he was laid out on the floor.

"With who, Jerricka? Nigga if you say Jerricka I'ma hit you right in yo shit."

"Hell no. That broad ain't settling down material. I don't know with who yet, I just know that's my plan." He shook his head, likely not believing me, but it was happening. I loved pops but I didn't want to end up alone like he did. He had us but it wasn't the same as having a mate.

"AND WHAT MAKES you a good candidate for this position?" I asked the fifth applicant that walked through Karmas. I already concluded that I wasn't hiring her based on her looks alone. She had a 27 piece weave, dressed like she was going to the club, and some long ass nails. The whole time she spoke I stared at her nails wondering how she wiped her ass with them. I was going to give her the decency of going through the whole interview process though.

"Well, I ain't never been no manager or nothing like that. Not in this type of setting anyway. I managed to get here though." She cracked up laughing at her weak joke while I stared at her with a straight face. "I'm just playing. I've only bartended at the previous club I worked at, but I'm sure I can get this manager thing figured out." She reached her hand across the table like she was gonna touch me and I pulled my hand back.

"Okay, you proved what doesn't make you a good candidate. Thank you for your time." I stood and waved my hand out to Jax to send the next person in.

"Wait, wait, that's it?" she asked clueless. "Damn, if I would've known the interview was going to waste my time, I wouldn't have brought my ass down here.

I was gonna let her off easy, but she had to say some slick shit. "Let me give you this tip for the future in case you go on any other interviews. First, be sure that your attire is appropriate. The first thing an employer takes note of is your appearance before you even open your mouth. You came in here today looking like you just came from the club or was on your way there. Lastly, answer the questions that are asked, not what you think is being asked. Have a good day Ms. Robinson."

She stood and stormed out, almost knocking the chair down. She was mad at me when all I was doing was giving her free game. I sat back down and pulled the next resume. Raven Clarke was the next interviewee. Skimming over her resume, I seen that she was co-manager at Ruth Chris steakhouse and front end manager at some other places. I wanted to hire her off the resume alone.

"Raven, this is Karma, Karma this is Raven," Jax announced. Taking my eyes off the paper in front of me, I looked up to find a chick dressed in a loose fitting pair of jeans, a pair of constructs and a polo button up. Shorty looked like she could be one of my niggas.

"How you doing Karma?" she held her hand out for me to shake. I obliged and her handshake was firm.

"Shit, you ain't nothing like I expected," I spoke honestly.

"Good, so I know fucking ain't on the table for the position," she replied smartly and made me laugh.

"Nah, shorty, nothing like that. I like my women more feminine," I assured her.

"We got something in common then. This is a nice place you got here."

"Preciate that. I read over your resume a little bit here. It's pretty impressive, especially for what I'm looking for."

"Thank you. As you can see, my last position was at Ruth Chris. They didn't appreciate what I brought to the table, so after two years I had to move on."

"Understood. Well for a GM at Karmas I need someone who can be me when I'm not around. You gotta be trustworthy and able to manage the different personalities I already have here. For the most part the staff is close knit and they're used to hearing my voice as boss. How would you go about ensuring that the staff understands and respects your position?"

"First, I'd meet with everyone and introduce myself. I'd make them aware that while I'll be their boss, I'm also a team player. Not to be confused with being a pushover though. You have to give respect to get it, and I plan on doing that."

I paused, allowing her answer to sink in before speaking. "I'ma take a chance on you. You have drive and you ain't gon' take no shit. I like that quality in a GM. Lets work." I held my hand out and she slapped it with a smile. I could tell Raven was gonna be a good hire.

6

AMANDA

I was stuck when I made it home and Aaron was asleep in the living room on the couch. My heart was beaten out of my chest because Kaiser had insisted on walking me to my door to ensure that I got in safely. Although I was still annoyed by the show the chick he was with put on, I thought it was cute that he wanted to make sure I was good. It was a good thing that once I got inside, he kept it pushing.

Now, I was sitting across from Aaron having dinner while he made pointless conversation. He had yet to get to the reason why he had been ignoring my calls. Shit, he hadn't even made an attempt to touch me since he'd been home the last 48 hours. It smelled a lot like some fuck shit in the air. I made sure to stab at the plate so that the sound would annoy him and he felt my aggression.

"You aight?"he finally asked, taking a sip of his jack and coke.

"No, I'm not," I replied aggressively. "I'm not aight Aaron. Do you wanna guess why?" I set my fork down and folded my hands on the table.

"Look, I'm sorry about not answering your calls while I was

out of town. You know when I'm on the go I'm focused on getting this money and keeping an eye out for the boys(police)."

I sat back in my chair and rolled my eyes hard. "You really think I'm going to let you slide with that weak ass excuse? It's no way that in the week you've been gone, you didn't pick up your phone not once to check up on me. Not only that, but you couldn't respond to a phone or text message? Since when did I get demoted to side bitch?" I needed answers.

"Here you go with the dramatics. Come on Manda, you know I'm out here tryna get this money," he tried to rationalize and I wasn't hearing it.

"And I'm not knocking you for doing that Aaron, I never have. It's become a problem here recently because our relationship has taken a backseat to your work. You've become more and more inconsiderate in the last few months." Irritated by his lack of empathy and delayed response, I got up, tossed the remainder of my food in the trash and went to my room.

I had never been a nagging woman and I didn't plan on starting today. I had a gut feeling that Aaron was on some bullshit, I just hadn't had the chance to go inspector gadget on his ass yet. That was the plan tonight though. As soon as his ass was good and tired, I planned to go through his phone. I wasn't doing anymore complaining, it was time for action.

"Manda," he called out to me. I sensed that he was at the bedroom door by how close his voice sounded. I didn't bother turning around to acknowledge him as I busied myself with pulling out a nightgown and underwear so that I could get ready for a shower. "Baby, don't act like that." He came up from behind me and kissed my neck.

"Move, Aaron." I pushed him back using little to no force. "Keep the same energy you had when you first got here." He didn't respond, but kept his lips on my neck, placing soft kisses along my collar bone. I hated him right now for knowing my weakness. I hadn't been touched in three weeks and two days, those subtle kisses made me whimper. He reached around and rubbed my pussy through my yoga pants, causing my love button to thump.

I needed the dick bad. Aaron knew what to do to shut me up. Lowkey I had the makings of a sex addict, but I maintained well. Slowly, he pulled at my pants. I helped by doing a little shimmy and stepped out of them using my feet. I was pantyless underneath, giving him easy access to my goodies. Spreading my legs open, his fingers moved like he was conducting a symphony making me bite my bottom lip.

"Mmmm," I moaned and matched his movements.

"I bet you this pussy missed me more than you did," he spoke in a low tone. I nodded my head yes. Any words I had were caught in my throat once he picked me up and sat me on top of my vanity. It's a good thing I didn't have anything on it. He put my legs in the crook of his arms and placed his face at my pussy. Inhaling my scent, he moaned before giving it a good licking.

I bucked against his mouth as he ate my pussy like he missed me. "Ooh, fuck, yes babe. Suck on that clit. Yeah, just like that." I grabbed the back of his head and held it against my clit and he didn't miss a beat. My clit thumped as he alternated between nibbling on it and sucking while sticking two fingers inside of me. "Uh, uh, I'm cummin," I yelled out while clamping my legs around his neck. The way my pussy squirted, I felt my hips cramp up. "Slide your dick inside", I requested, knowing my pussy was soaking wet. "No baby this was just about you" Aaron responded. Normally I would have protested, but I was really drained from the orgasm, so I lifted my leg over his head to stand and headed for the shower. My equilibrium was a little off, but I made it to the bathroom. In the shower, I thought about how I'd approach the situation if I did find anything suspicious in Aaron's phone. It was a toss up between fighting his ass or poisoning him. Either could land my ass in jail, but shit, at this point, I was willing to go.

Like I expected, after my shower, he was knocked out on the bed. Tightly wrapping my towel around my body, I walked back into the kitchen where he'd left his phone and picked it up off the table. It didn't take but two attempts to get the phone open and the first stop on my, "check this nigga list", was his text messages. My blood boiled seeing the multiple messages from me that he didn't even bother opening. Getting my mind right, I sat down and scrolled the messages for anything suspicious.

One that stood out in particular was a text thread between him and a woman named Terry. It was a lot of familiarity going on and a whole bunch of lol's and smiley faces. I had to scroll to the very beginning of the text thread to get a timeframe as to when it started. My hand went to my mouth to stifle my scream as I read the exchange between the two of them and my stomach felt weak. This motherfucka was telling this broad how much he was able to be himself when he's with her and how she completed him.

The nerve of this bastard to say he could be himself with someone else. I'd given Aaron the best years of my life, only to now feel like I'd been dealing with a stranger. I didn't need to read anymore. I slammed the phone down so hard the screen shattered. He wouldn't be making any late night calls to that bitch tonight. Walking back to the bedroom, I stood at the door watching him sleep peacefully. My first mind was to slap his ass awake, but I needed to process this before I made a move.

Snatching my pillow up from my side of the bed, I took my phone and started for the guest bedroom. It was no way I was sleeping next to his dog ass. I knew for sure only one of us would be waking up in the morning if I did. I tried fighting back tears, but as soon as my head hit the pillow they fell. It was one thing to think you're being cheated on, its another to have it confirmed. That fucked my head up. What made it even more sad was that I couldn't pinpoint where we went wrong. Even worse, I didn't know if we could get it back.

"AMANDA, AMANDA, GET UP MAN." Aaron shook me awake and I opened my eyes snatching back from him.

"Stop shaking me," I snapped and gave him an evil eye.

"What the hell happened to my phone Manda?" I got up and walked smooth past him and into the bathroom. I casually pulled down my panties to pee and he stood guard in the doorway. "Well?"he asked, still looking for answers.

"I smashed the screen after seeing messages between you and your main bitch," I answered smartly. Wiping myself, I flushed the toilet and went to the sink to wash my hands, making sure not to lose eye contact with him. His eyes showed that he was taken back by my honesty, although he tried not to convey it through his body language.

"It's not even like that Manda baby. You could've come and talked to me about the text." I wanted to know if he was aware of how dumb he sounded.

"Talk to you Aaron? Did you leave your mind at that bitch house?" I went to walk pass him and he blocked my path. "You need to move out of my way and right now. The way I'm feeling, I'll swing on your ass and we'll have to handle the rest later." I was hot and right about now, I needed to be far away from him.

"You see, I can't talk to you," he said to my back as I made it past him. I turned and stared him down.

"So that makes it okay for you to fuck around on me? What you're not gonna do is try and shift the blame and make your fuck up my fault. I've been nothing less than a good woman to you and you seem to have forgotten that. I'll tell you this though, I'm not about to fight for a position in your life. As far as I'm concerned, that bitch can have you." I left him standing there and he didn't bother following me.

Quickly throwing on a pair of jeans, t-shirt, and my Air Jordan Ones, I sent a text to Tracey asking if she was home. Setting my phone down, I put my shoulder length hair in a top knot and grabbed my purse. Checking to make sure all of my necessities were in place, I slipped a pair of underwear in there too. Depending on what the day might have in store, I may be in the mood for a little get back.

"That's what we doing now?" I turned and Aaron stood behind me with his arms folded.

"Go to hell Aaron." In my closet, I snatched my Balenciaga hoodie off the hanger and bumped him as I walked out. He had me confused with a silly bitch. My feelings were hurt more than anything and that was all the ammunition I needed for payback, if I wanted to go that route. Getting into my car, I checked my messages to see that Tracey had responded letting me know that she was home.

Letting her know I was on my way, I cruised towards her house. You know, usually when a woman gets cheated on, she often questions herself and what she could have done to keep her man. I wasn't gonna be one of them. I knew that there was nothing that I did to push Aaron into the arms of another woman. Picking up my phone as I stopped at the light, it began ringing and it was Kaiser calling.

"Hello Kaiser," I said in a dull tone.

"What's good bae?"

"I'am not your bae Kaiser."

"Are we gonna debate about that every time we speak?"

"Ughh, Kaiser what you want? Right now is not a good time."

"Tell me who made you mad so I can shoot they bitch ass." I don't know why the statement made me laugh but his silly ass did. "I don't know why you laughing. You should already know that I'm willing to go to war behind the woman I love." He threw the word love out there so easily. I immediately dismissed it.

"You real funny. Why are you calling me though?"

"I wanted to invite you out to breakfast."

"I'm not in the mood to eat right now. I got a lot on my mind."

"All the more reason why you shouldn't skip the most important meal of the day. Come fuck witcha boy and stop acting like that." I sighed and thought of every reason not to agree to this little outing. And he waited too.

"You know what, fine. I'll meet you." He told me to meet him at Row House in Harlem. I'd never been, but it wasn't too far from where I lived. It took me twenty minutes to get there and I had to park a block away. I sent a quick text to Tracey that I'd be by in a little bit and made sure to leave out that I was meeting up with Kaiser. That little piece of information, I planned to keep to myself. My phone chimed with a text message from him.

Kaiser: I'm inside, in the back.

Through the window, I could see him watching me. The place looked almost empty and I was cool with that. I didn't want to be amongst a bunch of people. I shook my head and opened the door. As I entered, the waitress directed me to the back as if she was expecting me.

"Good looking Gale. I'm gonna have my usual. You can give her a few minutes to look over the menu." He spoke for me and the waitress nodded her head before handing me my menu and walking off.

"This is a cute spot."

"Yeah, it's one of my go to's for breakfast. And you look good by the way," he complimented and kissed my cheek before I sat. I felt it tingle, but said nothing.

"I look like I'm on the go, but thank you for the compliment. I'm gonna have whatever you're having and a mimosa if they have them." Whatever they were cooking up in the kitchen, crept its way up front and into my nostrils. He waived the waitress over and gave her my order before focusing back on me.

"So wassup, who made you mad this morning?"

"I'm not about to discuss my life with you Kaiser." I would be crazy to admit that I had just found out that I was being cheated on not even twenty four hours ago.

"Okay, if you don't wanna talk about your present, I respect that. Let's talk about our future." He smiled and I admired his pretty white teeth that almost looked like veneers.

I leaned forward, so that he heard my next statement clearly. "We don't have a future."

"Are you happy?"he asked out of nowhere. I paused because I didn't know how to answer that question. Especially not at this very moment. I was taught to never talk down on my man to another man, no matter what we're going through. "You still here with me?"

"Oh, umm yeah. I drifted off for a minute. To answer your question, I'm good," I stated simply.

"So, you're content, got it."

"Excuse me?" I snapped with much attitude and a roll of my neck. "What's that supposed to mean?"

"Hey," he shrugged his shoulders, "you're the one who answered good. I'm going based off your response." I was about to give him a piece of my mind, but the food came. The scent was heavenly and the sautéed shrimp laid beautifully on the buttery grits. This was ten pounds that I was okay with putting on. I went to dig in and he stopped me.

"Nah, we gotta say grace." I lifted my head, shocked and he gestured for me to look down. What was going on here?

7

KAISER

I chuckled internally at the look on Amanda's face when I mentioned praying over our food. People always judged a gangsta when it had anything remotely to do with god. God was the homie and the reason I was still alive today. That I knew for sure. After thanking him for his many blessings and mercy, we both said amen. I lifted my head and she was still puzzled.

"You pray?"

"Is that a real question? God is the man, and he loves us all. Even the sinners such as myself."

"Oh, I wasn't judging like you just tried to do me a few seconds ago." I smirked at her feistiness.

"I wasn't judging you love. I made an observation. Let me say this, its not okay for you to be unhappy. Not when you've been with a nigga as long as you've been with homeboy. I've never been the type to throw dirt on the next mans name, but I see your value. I'm always going to put words to your thoughts."

"What does that even mean Kaiser?" I figured she'd be loss. Micah and Karma hated when I started talking my poetic shit and they couldn't keep up.

"I'm saying, the truth you're scared to reveal, I'm going to speak to that."

"Why don't you have a woman Kaiser? And don't try to mix your words or use me as the reason why." I studied her as she broke off a piece of her shrimp with her fork and mixed it with her grits. Delicately placing the fork to her mouth, the way she closed her eyes and savored the flavor made my dick hard. Underneath the table, I adjusted myself before answering.

"I'm single because can't nobody hold my interest long enough to be my woman. Also, word around the curb is," I leaned forward and whispered, "I'm a bit of an asshole."

"Say whatt??" She leaned back in her seat dramatically and we both laughed.

"So you think I'm an asshole too huh?"

"Sometimes, but you seem like you have a good heart." She winked at me and I shook my head. It didn't take me long to demolish my plate. The shrimp and grits were something to write home about. "I wanna open my pants so bad, but that would be so ghetto."

Amanda's giggle did something to my heart and that's how I knew she was the one. My concern wasn't the dude she was with because I had no problem putting that nigga on his ass if it came down to it. I knew she was settling and so did she. Being around her on different occasions I often took note of her eyes. The twinkle that was once there had been dim lately. I wanted to be the one to put that spark back.

"You can be yourself when you're with me bae," I assured her.

"Hmph, I heard that before," she scoffed and rolled her eyes.

"Do tell."

"Nope, I've said enough. Thank you for breakfast Kaiser." Going into her purse, she pulled out a ten dollar bill and placed it on the table. "This is a tip for Gale."

"I already paid her, but I'll make sure she gets it." She leaned over to hug me and I held her around her waist, putting my face in her neck.

"I'm gonna make you mines. I let you slip away from me too many times. Know that I'm coming for my wife." Kissing her neck, I let her go. She pulled back slowly and I stared into her soul, so that she knew that I meant every fucking word. "Let me walk you to your car." I went to stand and she shook her head no.

"Uh, uh, I'm straight." Turning quickly, she left the restaurant and I laughed lightly.

"You wearing her down son," Gale commented as she walked over to clean off the table.

"I know. You're gonna be seeing a lot of her around here. Thanks for the food and as always, your service."

"Yeah, you know you're the only one that can get me to put on my chef hat and get back in the kitchen. You stay safe out there Kaiser." She gave me a soft smile and I left.

I SAT at a table inside one of the apartments we used for money collection only and looked on as Jeff counted the pile of money on the table. Jeff was in charge of making sure the money was straight before I came through to collect it. When he went to count the money for the third time, I stopped him.

"Dawg, counting it a third time ain't gon' magically make the count right. It's short two bands. I counted it with you the first time. Tell me something because I'm getting claustrophobic in this bitch."

"Kaiser, man, Ron was the last person to drop off his bag tonight." I stared, waiting for him to continue. "I had just ate some tacos before he got here so I told him to drop his bag and I'd hit him once the count was done. Then you happened to show up, just as I was setting up to count and his bag is the only one that's short."

"So, what you saying is, you let that man come in sit the bag down and leave? You didn't have him wait until you came off the pot?" As I spoke, I pulled one of my best friends from my waist. My .45 was too pretty, shining and shit.

"I wasn't thinking man, I'm sorry. Look, I can put the money back and then square it away with Ron later." He frantically went to reach for his pocket and I let off a shot that hit him in the hand.

"What the fuck!"he yelled out, grabbing his hand to stop it from leaking.

"Keep your voice down before you disturb the peace around here and I really have to make a scene. Now, you know better than to even come to me with any stories about why shit is not straight. You're the last person to touch the money before it gets to me, so it's your responsibility to make sure shit is straight. No fucking excuses dawg. Go wrap that shit up and get the fuck outta here. You on leave with no pay, pending review."

He scurried off and I grabbed the black duffle bag that sat on the table and started to put the money inside. I couldn't believe this motherfucka. I didn't tolerate fuck ups because niggas had been around me long enough to know how I ran things. His fuck up would cost him and Ron. It took him a few minutes before he returned with his hand in a towel.

"Run that two bands my guy." Reaching into the same pocket as earlier as best as he could he pulled out a wad of cash. Taking it from him, I took the money owed and handed him back the rest. "Straighten up ya walk before we leave outta here. I don't want all that attention on me." Picking up the duffle bag, I headed towards the door with him behind me. After ensuring he got in his car, I threw the bag in my trunk and sped off to Grant in search of Ron.

I texted Micah while driving to let him know that we needed a new money man and that I'd see him shortly. I slowly rolled through Grant Projects and spotted Ron chilling in one of the parks. My burnt orange BMW 650 stood out like a sore thumb, so I'm sure people were tryna figure out who I was through my tints. Although they were looking, no one approached the car. Rolling down the window, I called out Ron's name. Of course he didn't immediately walk over to the car. I beeped the horn and called his name again, lowering the window full so that my face was on display.

"Shit, wassup Kaiser. What you doing on this side?"

"Go let ya people know we closing down shop early tonight in this building and then come back over." He looked baffled, but did as I asked.

"Everything aiight?" He asked when he returned back to the car.

"Nah, it ain't and I'm sure you know that. You owe me something and I'ma need that like right now."

"Huh?"he questioned nervously. Not in the mood for the silly shit, I put the gun on the dashboard and turned towards him.

"I'm not gonna play this game witchu Ron. Don't make it worse than it already is. Come up off that bread sir."

"Dawg, let me explain. It was just a miscount and I was gonna get back to Jeff tonight," he talked while going in his pockets and pulling out cash. Snatching it all from him, I put it in the center console.

"Nah, it wasn't no miscount. Had I not shown up here you would've went about your evening. And you know what happens to thieves right Ron?"

"Kaiser, please man, I'm not bullshitting you." His pleas fell on death ears.

"Exit my car, someone will be seeing you shortly. And if you run, you know you'll have to see Micah at the House of Horrors."

I could see the tears well up in the corners of his eyes, but I felt no sympathy for him. There was no place for him in the crew anymore. "You can go sit in the park." Hanging his head, he got out and walked back in the park. I sent a message to my boy Demon and let him know that someone needed to be wheel chaired. When you went against me, I made it so that I didn't kill you, but you lived everyday to regret your decision. Driving off, I headed to Micah's crib to drop the bag off.

En route, I sent a text to Amanda to let her know that I was thinking about her. She sent back a smiley face emoji and that was good enough for me. Before I could put it down, the phone rang in my hand as I pulled onto Micah's street, it was Ariane. I hadn't spoken to her since she showed her ass at Karma's a few nights ago. I picked up, but said nothing.

"Hello, Kaiser?"

"Wassup Ariane?"

"You tell me, I haven't heard from you in a few days. You acting brand new now?"

"Nah, I had to let you cool off because the last time I was in your presence, I didn't like what I saw. You were on some other shit." Typing in the code to the gate, it opened and I drove in. Parking in the winding driveway, I got out and grabbed the duffle bag from the trunk.

"I hear what you saying, but you have to admit it was disrespectful for you to have been dry fucking the next chick in my face. I mean, you invited me out."

"I did, but I'm not your man. We just fucking. I thought we were very clear on that."

"Okay, we're not just fucking. We spend time together too, don't do that."

"Ariane, we fuck and we chill. Please don't start reading too much into that because you'll only end up hurt at the end of the day. Hit me up when you figure out your emotions. I gotta go." I hung up the phone and before I could knock on the door, Eniko stood behind it smiling.

"What's good, uncle Kaiser?"she imitated me and we both laughed.

"Wassup gangsta, what you doing here?"

"What you mean? I live here."

I laughed again while walking inside. "I mean you're not usually here when I come by. I was starting to miss ya kiddo."

"Oh, that's cause I'ma busy woman."

"And about to be a grounded woman if you don't get in that room and clean it up Ms.Thang," Kelly said from behind her. MJ hung off her hip as usual.

"Oop, I gotta go unc. I'ma holla at you." She jetted off and Kelly shook her head laughing.

"That little girl is a trip, hey Kaiser."

"Wassup sis, this lil nigga getting chunky."

"Language!"she said in a white voice while covering MJ's ears and pulling him back.

"My bad, my bad. Where yo dude at?" She pointed toward the back, letting me know he was in his man cave. I headed back that way. I did the signature knock and he let me in. Opening the door he gave me a questioning look that I returned.

"I wanted to see if you had any blood splatter on you."

"These Timbs is fresh out the box. If a nigga get any blood on these, I gotta whip his ass. Besides, my mood is real relaxed, so I used my gun today."

"On who?"

"Jeff, for being irresponsible. And Demon had to wheelchair Ron for having sticky fingers. I'll have the replacements in both spots first thing in the morning." I handed him the duffle bag and sat down.

"What got you in a good mood?"

"I had breakfast with the wife this morning. She didn't give me too many problems about it either."

"Amanda finally gave you an hour of her time huh?"

"Yeah, and I gotta get my baby man. My girl ain't happy, I can tell. Like she's crying out for me on some Mario shit. That nigga on borrowed time."

"So you gon kill her dude?"he asked, smirking.

"That nigga gon' kill hisself once I snatch Manda up and put twins in her."

"I'm not even gon get into that conversation witchu. All I can say is good luck, playboy." I didn't need luck, plans were already in motion.

"WHAT ARE YOU DOING HERE VIV?" I heard my dad ask someone in the middle of the night. I'd just woken up to take a piss and overheard a conversation taking place in the kitchen, prompting me to get closer to listen.

"You missed your scheduled payment this month and I came to find out why." It was a woman's voice. I wanted to know who was so bold as to come to our house and question my pops. Koran was a crazy motherfucka and not too many would have the audacity.

"You know better than to even be around here questioning me. And keep your voice down before you wake up my sons. As far as those payments go, it's a wrap". I wanted to laugh at the exchange, but the chuckle got caught in my throat when the woman spoke again.

"You're right, those are your sons, but I'm the bitch that pushed them out, because your half righteous ass wouldn't let me abort them, knowing they was going to fuck up my figure and tie me down. Now you agreed to pay me my child support as long as I did that and stayed away and ive done both so a bitch need her coins!"

"Viv the only reason I asked you to stay away was because you have made it clear that you don't want to be a mother to them boys and I ain't about to let you come into their lives if you aint ready to love them the way they deserve. Both of them are so

smart and Kaiser has your sense of humor. But your ass rather run these streets. think I hear about the shit you out here doing?!

"Koran what I'm out here doing ain't none of your fucking business, I didn't come here for none of your Muslim mother woman shit, I came to get my money!

"You really are a sorry Bitch, that's your response to being in your children's life? I shouldn't have given you shit and I'll tell you this, you won't see another dime from me and that's on Kaiser and Karma."

"You know what Koran, I knew this shit was going to happen once I had them boys, everything was going to come down to them first. This is exactly why I didn't want to do it. Fuck you I don't need your money. I'm still a bad bitch, with no kids out here, I'll find someone with a big bag. You just make sure you stay out of what I got going on and I'll stay away from you and yours!"

" Get outta my house before I forget you're a woman." I peeked around the corner and tried to get a good look at the woman who'd abandoned Karma and I. Unfortunately, I only saw the back of her head as my pops forced her out. He slammed the door so hard I was surprised Karma didn't wake up.

That night the discontent for my mother quickly festered and turned into hate. My lack of love from her may have played a part in why I didn't want to settle down. Well that and I simply just didn't love these hoes. Amanda was the one though and everything I lacked to the outside world, I was reserving it for her.

8

DOMINIQUE

"Sorry, sorry, sorry I'm late. I had a consultation with a client that ran way over schedule." I made my way into the boardroom where we were holding our monthly meeting. I didn't do late, so I was annoyed that all eyes were on me when I walked through the door and to my seat across from Kelly.

"You good D," Micah assured. "We were going over the listings for the month. By the way, congrats on your million dollar closing. "The room erupted in applause and Kelly winked her eye at me.

"Y'all know how I do," I joked and everyone laughed. "No, but thank you. It was hard, but I got it done."

"Another one for the books. Let's see if you can make it happen again." Micah handed me a listing for a loft in Soho. It was a cool 1.5 million. The place was breathtaking to say the least. I went through the presentation booklet that he put together with the clients information and brief overview of the listing. I thought my eyes were deceiving me when I saw Karma's name on the paperwork. I must've been zoned out too because when I looked up everyone was filing out of the office except for Micah and Kelly.

"Well, I'm glad they're gone so I can cuss you out Micah," I scolded him. He tried to keep a straight face, but ended up smirking.

"What happened?" Kelly asked clueless. I thought she was covering for him, but by the questioning look on her face I knew she wasn't.

"This loft is for Karma, that's what happened." Micah laughed and Kelly punched him in his arm.

"Babe, you know you wrong for that," Kelly let him know and I concurred. This smelled like a set up

"Why you beating up on me? He's a client and he requested the best, so I set him up with the best agent on my team."

"Oh, I'm not offended," Kelly said with a playful roll of her eyes. Micah leaned over and kissed her cheek.

"And you have no reason to be my love. Karma specifically asked for Domonique. I'm sure you can get past whatever issue you may have. If you're not cool with it I can give the listing to one of the guys."

"Oh my god," I sulked and pouted like a child.

"You betta go get that money and stop playing boo."

"I'ma do that for sure. Micah, talk to ya friend and tell him to keep it strictly professional."

"Done." I got up and went into my office to do my own research on the property. I liked to be overly prepared. Unfortunately for me, my mind drew a blank soon as I unlocked my computer. My mind was on being in Karma's presence again and how not in control I felt when I was around him. The last time I'd seen him was when he was at my front door. To say that I was shocked was an understatement. After I politely turned him away, I spent the remainder of my day thinking about what would've happened had I let him inside.

"Hey girl, is it okay if I come in?" Kelly asked through my cracked door.

"Of course." She came in and closed the door behind her. "How do you really feel about going on this showing? It's just between me and you."

"Honestly, I can't help but to think it's a set up. I don't like how my body reacts when I'm in Karma's presence. I mean, I've been around him multiple times but never one on one besides when he drove me home a couple nights ago. Girl, do you know he popped up at my house the next day like he wanted to kick it."

"Oh no he didn't," she said giggling.

"Girl, yes, showed up with a smile and all."

"And what you do?" She sat on the edge of her seat as if I was gonna tell her some big secret. I laughed at how wide her eyes got.

"Back up girl. I told him to leave."

"What?"

"I told him to leave. That was so awkward for him to show up unannounced. Not that I thought that he'd do anything to me, but still—"

"You wanted him to," she said cutting me off and giggling some more.

"Get out my office Kelly." I laughed along with her and she got up, shrugging her shoulders.

"I'm just saying Karma look like he'll crack that back just right."

"Out!" She was in a fit of laughter making her way out the door.

"Okay, okay, I'm sure he'll be on his best behavior during the showing."

"Hmph, he better be. Matter fact, I'm gonna send him a text to see if we can meet up today. The sooner I can get this place sold, the better."

"Well, good luck boo. Who knows, maybe they'll be some sparks between you two."

"Yep, from my taser if he get outta pocket." I wasn't playing, I'd fry Karma cute ass right up.

I SAT in my car outside of the building awaiting Karma's arrival. He was ten minutes late and I was ready to put my professional hat to the side and curse his ass out as soon as he pulled up. I specifically told him how I felt about tardiness when I texted him to meet with me. I was serious about my work and I didn't like to wait on anyone, especially when they didn't send a courtesy call or text. Just as I was about to text him a Jaguar F-Type pulled up next to me and the window rolled down slowly. I immediately recognized Karma behind the wheel.

"You're late," I said with an attitude.

"I know beautiful and I'm sorry about that." Karma didn't look like the type to apologize so I accepted it, but it did little to settle my annoyance.

"Okay, you can park in front of me and we can go in and see the place."

"I'd rather park behind you." I caught the flirty comment and ignored it. He chuckled and rolled his window up before parking in front like I asked him to. I watched as he stepped out of his car and I got all tingly inside. Like his brother, Karma's hair was dreaded but his weren't dyed.

The name brand jeans he had on hung slightly off his waist exposing his Ethika boxers. He sported a white crew neck t-shirt and his neck tattoo was on full display. Dammit, why he had to be so damn fine. I didn't know if he caught me admiring him through my front window, but I started moving to get out once he started walking toward my car. As he approached, I put the paperwork in my bag and went to open the door.

"I got it," I said, opening the door as he reached for the handle.

"Okay, independent woman." I rolled my eyes and hopped down out of my truck. He followed close behind me as I crossed the street. From the outside, it looked like any other normal apartment building, but opening the door and entering the main floor, you could tell it was anything but that.

"As you can see, this well laid out traditional loft complete with double height ceilings epitomizes quintessential loft living," I spoke while walking through the 2,452 square foot home. The pictures did the place no justice. It took an hour to tour the whole house because I wanted him to see everything it had to offer.

"Yeah, this is tough. I especially like the open space. All of this is newly renovated?"

"Yep, the previous owners did renovations last year."

"I don't know if you noticed that baby grand piano back in the great room. Do they plan on taking that or is it up for sale too?"

"I'm not sure. He's a music producer, so I think he'd want it. I'll inquire about it though. Are you leaning towards making an offer on it?"

"Oh yeah, I'm sold. I need to ask one more thing—

"Let me stop you right there," I cut him off with my hand up, "All I'm interested in is selling this loft."

"You too beautiful to be so hostile. What I was gonna ask before you cut me off was can I have all the furniture removed before my move in date. I'm not into hand me downs."

"Oh, umm, okay cool. I have the paperwork here for you to sign." I pulled out the manilla folder, set it on the kitchen counter, and tried poorly to recover from the embarrassment by rushing him to sign. By jumping the gun, I stuck my foot in my mouth and I knew by now Karma was over me. I was so rattled, I found myself mixing papers and getting frustrated.

"Aye, take a deep breath beautiful." He was now invading

my personal space. My body stood frozen and my heart felt like it was beating out of my mouth. I felt his breath on my neck and my hairs stood up.

"Can you give me a few feet? You playing me a little too close." My lips spoke the words, but my body was feeling differently.

"You got that." He stepped back enough for me to breathe easy. "Where do I sign?" I went through everything with him and we closed the deal. "Can I ask you a question?"

"Does it have anything to do with this place?"

"Nah."

"Then no, you can't ask me a question." I signed my part of the paperwork and gathered everything so that I could leave.

"I wanna know who hurt you."

"Excuse me?" My lip curled up as I grilled him. How dare he ask me such a personal question. "Nobody hurt me. Where did you get that I was hurt by me telling you can't ask me a question?"

"If you give me a chance to talk to you, you'd see that I'm not coming from a bad place," he spoke genuinely. His tone never changed even though mines was giving every bit of bitch. "You look like you could use some love. I'm almost positive that behind that smile that you usually have plastered on your face there's a heart that needs mending. And a nigga ain't tryna feed you no lines either. I do know a hurt woman when I see one. Thank you for the tour. Right now, I gotta make a move. Meet me at my club later with the keys."

He left me standing there without giving me a chance at a rebuttal. A part of me wanted to tell him that he was right, I had been hurt. I've been hurting ever since my parents died, but I had no one to cry to. Now that I had friends like Kelly and Amanda, I was able to express myself more. I hadn't gone into my life story with them yet, but we were building a bond to where if they asked, I'd feel comfortable telling them.

I cut my feelings off completely from men and only used them for company when I was bored or my toy wasn't cutting it. Other than that, I could do without the headache or heartache. Karma seemed like he came with a lot of heartache, yet still I found myself drawn to the man. Shaking my head, I scrolled through my contacts in my phone and my finger hovered over the number for my therapist. I hadn't seen her in a few weeks and right now I needed someone to talk to.

Me: Hey Nina, do you have any openings today? I could use a face to face.

Doc Nina: Sure, are you available to come in now?

Me: Yes, I'll see you shortly.

I never thought that I'd be the girl that would even consider therapy, but I could admit that talking to Nina was good for me. I'd had a one on one with myself and came to the conclusion that I needed to speak to someone in order to sort out my feelings. I went out on a whim and googled therapists near me and God sent me Nina. She was patient from day one and didn't pressure me into talking, I went at my own pace. Today, I wanted to hear that it was okay to allow Karma to get to know me.

"It's good to see you Domonique. You've been hiding from me," Nina said as I entered her office.

I laughed and gave her a hug. "I haven't been hiding, I've been busy. I'm actually just coming from a showing."

"Okay, I'll let you pass with the busy line. How's everything going outside of work?"

"Good, for the most part. I've been hanging out with Kelly and Amanda a lot."

"Good for you, anything happening in your love life?"

I shook my head. "Nope, still non existent and I like it that way."

"Domonique."

"Ughh, okay, I'm still lonely as hell Nina. What's wrong with me?"

"Nothing is wrong with you. You've built up a wall that's almost impossible for anyone to penetrate. You're scared of loving and losing; again." I knew she was referring to my parents. That was a loss that I still had yet to get over. I don't think I ever will.

"There's this guy though. He seems interesting to want to get to know."

"Well look, see, we're getting somewhere. Tell me a little bit about this guy." I involuntarily smiled thinking about Karma.

"I can't tell you much. We haven't hung out alone yet. He's been hinting at it though."

"Dominique, I think you should give him a chance. Let him take you out and show you a good time. Who knows, it might even lead to something else." She winked her eye and I caught her drift.

"Oh no you didn't," I snickered. "I do just fine with what I have, thank you."

"It's just a suggestion. Seriously though, the next time he hints at wanting to take you out, oblige him."

"I'll think about it, but I won't make any promises."

9

KARMA

Ever since I handed over the reigns of the day to day dealings at the club to Raven, things had been moving smoothly. As she suggested, we had a meeting with the staff to introduce her and everyone seemed on board. She had even developed her own little fan club amongst the female staff. Like I mentioned before, Raven walked and talked like one of the homies. It was a smooth transition overall. Getting out of my car, I made my way inside the lounge. I had to cut my meeting with Domonique short due to today being inventory day at the club.

The place Micah found for me was just my speed. It was fit for a king, and if Domonique played her cards right she could be apart of it. It was cool seeing her in her element as she walked me through the loft, giving details of what made each room unique. Having prior business at the lounge couldn't have come at a better time. It gave me an excuse to leave knowing she would have to meet me again to give me the keys. Using my finger print, I entered through the back door of the lounge. My phone vibrated in my pocket and it was Raven calling.

"I know you calling to let me know you're on your way

right?" I wasn't a fan of excuses and being late was a pet peeve of mines.

"Man, you ain't gon' believe this shit. I was headed your way and I had to make a quick stop at the bank to check my safety deposit box. Why I get in this bitch and these crackers acting like they didn't wanna give me access to my own shit. I went off so bad, I knew I was close to getting my black ass locked up."

"Well, did they let you into the box?" I laughed, awaiting her response.

"Hell yeah! Talking bout they apologize and have a new security protocol. Them motherfuckas had me fucked up behind my bread. I'm almost to you though."

"Aight, I'll be in the back." We hung up and I headed back to my office. Our delivery trucks were set to arrive soon and I wanted to go over the copies for the orders I'd made. I was a business man at heart so I fell into the role of business owner quickly. I made sure my business ran smoothly and I didn't cut corners. As I sat down at my desk, my phone went off again, this time it was my brother.

"Wassup fool."

"Yo, why the fuck are these edible arrangements so damn expensive bro?"

I couldn't help but laugh at him. This dude was so cheap with the smallest things. "Who ya cheap ass buying edible arrangements for?"

"My future wife nigga, keep up."

"How much is the arrangement Kaiser?" I asked, annoyed.

"With tax it came out to $120. They tryna break a nigga."

"Bro, you bitching about 120 when you just spent that on a Gucci tee in a minute."

"This is fruit we talking about though Karma. Fruit in a little cute ass bowl. If it wasn't for my lady, I wouldn't even be on this damn site."

"Man, just buy the damn fruit witcho crazy ass. What else you got going on today?

"You know me, I'ma play the streets for a bit, then do a little shopping for the trip." I missed being in the trenches and being out there with my twin. We could hold our own, but the two of us out there was dynamic.

"Aight, come through the lounge tonight and have a celebratory drink with ya brother tonight."

"What we celebrating? Ahh man, they found a cure for the herpes that chick gave you from Uptown?" He laughed hard as if he'd said the funniest joke.

"Nigga, don't play with me like that. This dick ain't never been burning, pause. We celebrating my new crib. I closed on it today with the help of Domonique."

"Ooh, aight. My boy doing anything just to be in Domonique presence huh? I see you playa."

"Man, whatever. I'll see you later."

"Aight, love."

"Love." That was our way of telling each other I love you without saying the full statement. Through the security camera, I could see Raven enter the building and went out to meet her. I wanted to have all of the inventory stocked before we opened. With the two of us, it'd take awhile, but it would get done correctly.

I NEED ya body in ways, that you don't understand, but I'm losing my patience. Cause' we been going over and over again. Girl I just wanna take you home, and get right to it. Chris Brown's "Privacy" played throughout the club as people started to file in. I sat up in VIP and watched everything from the balcony. There wasn't a day where Karma's was open and we didn't have a packed house.

The atmosphere and hospitality was what kept people coming back. I scanned the crowd, in search of one face in particular. Domonique had texted me earlier, letting me know to expect her soon. Checking the time on my AP, it was nearing ten. Just as I went to send Domonique a text, she beat me to it.

Domonique: Can you come down and tell this overgrown security guard to let me upstairs before I kick him in the balls?

Me: Lol, give my dude a break, he's new. I'm coming down now.

I chuckled and headed for the steps. Alan was the security guard she was referring to. He'd just started last week and dude was strict as hell. If you didn't have a VIP reservation that nigga wasn't letting you cross the threshold. He didn't care if you were the president. I walked out of VIP and tapped him on his shoulder. Pointing to a frustrated Domonique, I let him know she was good to come up. He apologized to her, and let her know he was just doing his job.

"Yeah, whatever. Excuse me, Biz Markie." He moved to the side and she sauntered up the steps.

"You got a live one on your hands there," he commented with a smirk.

"You don't even know the half man. My brother will be pulling up in a few as well, let him up."

"I got you." I hope he didn't try to pull the same stunt he pulled with Domonique on Kaiser. He'd be quitting before I could even think about firing him. I followed behind all of the ass in front of me and took notice of Domonique's attire. She'd changed from the professional clothing she had on and now had on a black, mid length black dress that was tailored to her bountiful curves.

"Stop staring at my ass Karma. Let's finish this final transaction sir."

"Okay, meany. Where you in a rush to?" I asked trying to stall just so I could be in her presence a little while longer.

"Well, if you must know, I'm going downstairs to the bar to get a drink on you," she pointed at me and took a seat. Setting her Hermes bag on the table, she pulled out an envelope and handed it to me. Inside held the paperwork for my new place along with a set of keys. "Congrats."

"Thank you for coming down to hand deliver these beautiful." I took a seat across from her and moved the folder to the side. "What you drinking?"

"I'll let the bartender know once I get back downstairs."

"Why be downstairs amongst all those people when you can chill up here? I'll make a call and have your drink of choice sent up."

"I want some wings too. And top shelf me baller."

"I got you beautiful." I got up to place the order through the intercom on the wall and watch her as she typed on her phone. Domonique had a dope aura about her. This was my chance to get to know her a little better. I put in the order and made sure to request that Raven bought it up. Although I hadn't mixed business with pleasure with the women I employed, it didn't stop them from propositioning me whenever they got the chance.

"I love the atmosphere here. You did a good job of bringing everything together. I remember when the place was empty."

"My first compliment from you, we getting somewhere. Thank you, I couldn't have done it without E Luxe finding the perfect property for me."

"You know how we do." She smiled and patted herself on the back.

"I wanna get to know you D. On some friend shit to began with of course."

She leaned forward and crossed her hands on the table. "What you wanna know Karma, my dreams, my fears?" She was sarcastic in her response.

"I wanna know your favorite color," I countered.

"My favorite color?" I shook my head yes. "Umm, my favorite color is yellow."

"And your favorite movie?" I went down the list of favorite questions until I got to asking her favorite position.

"See, that's where I have to stop you. You just slid that one in there."

I laughed aloud and she kept a straight face. "Aight, I was just fucking witchu. I know a little more about you now." A knock on the door let me know that the food had finally arrived. It wasn't Raven delivering the food as I requested though.

"Thank you Bianca," I said as I took the tray from her.

"You're welcome boss man. Would you like some company?" She flashed all thirty twos and swiped her tongue over her top lip.

"Nah, I'm straight." Catching my drift, she turned around and walked back down the steps.

"Your little admirer could've just dropped my food off and y'all could've gone somewhere else to make googly eyes somewhere else." I caught the roll of Domonique's eyes as I placed the food in front of her.

"Googly eyes?" I mocked her. "I don't fraternize with the staff."

"Uh huh, I'll believe that the day you do. Ohhh, this is my song." She threw her hands in the air and swayed her hips in the seat while Tory Lanez "B.I.D" played in the room. I sat across from her and watched her rap the song word for word. I don't know why, but the scene was sexy as fuck.

"You want me to tell the DJ to run it back?"

She smirked, "nah, that was good enough for me. I need to get to these wings. What y'all put on these joints, some special kinda sauce or something?"

"That's a secret and if I tell you, you gotta let me take you out on a date."

Smiling, she took a bite of one of her wings and closed her eyes to savor the flavor. "Mmm, so good. Why you wanna take me out on a date Karma?"

"Why not?" I questioned her odd question. Picking up her napkin, she wiped her mouth dainty and placed it back on the table.

"Okay, let's do it. Just so you know, I don't like corny stuff. If you don't plan on showing up as yourself, stay home." There was no need to respond because I wasn't no corny ass nigga. I was going to show up as me every time. Domonique was gonna wish she said yes sooner.

AMANDA

I walked into work today, with the mindset that today was gonna be a good day. I hadn't spoken to Aaron in the last forty eight hours, and although it pissed me off, I wasn't gonna let it continue to keep me down. As I walked through the shop, all eyes were on me. That was usually the case, but today I saw mostly smirks from Diamond's minions, and genuine smiles from the stylist I fucked with. And that was only three people. Making my way over to my station, I was able to see why.

There was a huge bouquet of red roses, and a big edible arrangement sitting at my booth. A smile formed on my face, that I couldn't even hide. I already knew who the flowers, and fruits were from without even having to check the little card that stuck out of it.

"Ain't your boyfriend name Aaron?" Diamond asked from the booth next to me. Of course the bitch wanted to be messy.

"Shouldn't you be up front, answering a phone or some- thing?" I countered with much attitude.

"Girl, you don't even have to do all that. I only asked because I was the one who accepted the package for you. The guy mentioned it was from Kaiser, so I figured he was delivering to the wrong person, but do you." She spun around in her chair, so that her back was facing me.

I could have responded, and told the bitch to mind her business, but like I said, I was gonna have a good day today. Picking up the arrangement, I walked to the back to put them in the fridge. As I passed my homegirl Yvonne's station, she winked her eye at me, and popped her mouth. I chuckled, and kept it moving toward the back. The arrangement was so pretty. The strawberries, kiwi, oranges, grapes, and cantaloupe looked so fresh, I couldn't help but to set the vase down, and pick at it. After picking off what I wanted, I removed the card to read it before placing the fruits in the fridge.

This expensive ass arrangement was sent to a beautiful woman, who will soon be my beautiful wife. Thank you for taking the time out, and letting me treat you to some breakfast. I know we didn't spend much time together, but I hope that hour left a lasting impression on you. Now, the next thing we have to conquer is dinner. I don't want you wearing that sexy ass shit you wore at the club the other night, but I still want you to be sexy. Anyway, my damn hand starting to hurt, so I hope this package did what it was intended to make you do; smile. Forever your Man, Kaiser.

I couldn't help but to laugh and be over him at the same time. Kaiser was very rare. The words usually just came out of his mouth, just the way they came out on this paper. It was starting to grow on me, and make me feel some type of way. Placing the card back into the small envelope, I pulled out my phone to call him. Just as I went to select his contact, a call from Aaron came through. The call threw me off guard, so I quickly declined it.

I didn't expect to hear from him, and quite frankly, I didn't want to. Selecting his name, I sent a text letting him know that I was busy. To my surprise, he texted back immediately, saying that he was home, and would see me when he got off work. Aaron had me so fucked up. I wasn't playing with his ass this time. I didn't even bother responding. Now that I knew he was home, I was gonna make plans not to be. Exiting out of the text, I called Kaiser.

"Wassup bae,"he answered on the first ring.

I smiled, but corrected him. "I am not your bae, Kaiser."

"Aight, wassup boo. Did you get my package?"

"I did, and I was calling to say, thank you. I really appreciate it."

"No problem. Them hoes was in there hating, wasn't they?"

I laughed, and nodded my head as if he could see me. "You know I don't pay them broads no mind. Let me let you go though. I have a client coming in a few, and I wanna get ready for him."

"Him?"

"Yes, him. I do have male clients, Kaiser."

"Whats's that nigga name? Matter fact, send me a picture of him when he get there."

"Bye, Kaiser." I laughed, and went to hang up the phone. This man was a trip.

"Wait, I was gonna ask you this later, but since you called, might as well do it now. How do you feel about coming out to dinner with me tonight? It won't just be me, and you either. Micah, and Tracey will be there, and I believe Karma invited y'all girl Domonique."

"Sure, what time?"

"Oh, word? Just like that, I get a yes. I gotta start sending yo' ass expensive fruit baskets more often. I'll be by to pick to pick you up at around eight." Remembering that Aaron was home, I quickly nixed that idea.

"Meet me at Micah's, I'm gonna get ready there." I put the phone on speaker, and went to text Kelly to ask if it was okay if I came over tonight. She responded immediately, telling me to stop asking her silly questions.

"Aight, I'll see you then bae." I disconnected the call, and went to start my long work day. I was hoping that my night ended well.

INSTEAD OF GOING HOME, I decided to hit Saks to find me a quick outfit for dinner tonight. I didn't wanna do too much, and not because I was listening to Kaiser either. I was in, and out in under thirty minutes. That was a breaking record for me because I could easily be in Saks for two hours taking my time with my selections. As I went to walk out, I could see the chick that was with Kaiser at the lounge entering with another female. She stared hard at me, but I wasn't into petty female exchanges, so I kept it moving.

"Yea, girl, that's ol' girl that was tryna push up on Kaiser at Karmas. I had to check her ass real quick. You know I'm not about to play with no bitch about my man." Her, and the other female slapped fives, making me shake my head. I could've embarrassed her by calling Kaiser up to confirm our dinner date tonight, but decided against it. She wasn't gonna get away with calling me out of my name tho. Hell would have to freeze over before I let anyone get away with disrespecting me.

"Excuse me," I called out, and she turned around. "Yea, you," I pointed to her, "you're a little too old to be out here making up false narratives aren't you? I mean, you look old enough to know better. Please do me a favor, and be careful with that bitch word when referring to me. The only reason why I haven't knocked you into that clothing rack is because I frequent this establishment often. However, if you'd like to step outside, and discuss your man, we can do that."

I wanted her to jump stupid, so I could tear her ass up. I hadn't had a fight in a while, but I'd come out of retirement real quick. Her friend must've seen the seriousness in my face because she made the decision for her, by pulling her away. It be the bitches with the most mouth that don't really be with the static. I kept it moving, leaving the store with a slight attitude.

I couldn't wait to see Kaiser. I was gonna curse him out just for one of his hoe's thinking they could play with me. This was the reason why a dude like Kaiser wasn't for me. Jumping in my car, I connected my phone to the bluetooth, and called Tracey. I hadn't checked in with her since we were out to eat. The phone rang twice before she answered.

"Hey, boo, what's going on?" She spoke into the phone all jovial and shit.

"Hey, cousin, I was just calling in to check on you. What you up to?"

"Still drug free."

I laughed at her statement. I couldn't hide that I check in on her more than often just to make sure that she didn't relapse. She knew it too, but answered the phone for me anyway. She knew for a fact that I wouldn't hesitate to do one of my pop ups if she didn't.

"I know that's right. I need your advice on something real quick tho." I figured I'd run the whole Kaiser situation down to her to see what she thought about it. When I did, I could hear clapping on her end.

"Who the hell is clapping?"

"Girl, me," she snickered. "So when you gon' drop Aaron? I'm tired of pretending that I like him."

"Girl, what?" I bust out laughing at her reaction. "You have not been pretending."

"Oh yes the hell I have. It's always been something about him that just didn't sit right in my soul. I wanted to give you the opportunity to figure that out tho."

"I'm not leaving him tho, Tracey. At least at the moment." I'd given most of my life to Aaron, I didn't wanna just up, and throw it away.

"Oh, you're leaving, you just haven't thought it through yet.

The moment you got on this phone talking to me about another man, you made your decision, boo."

I thought about it for a minute, and what she said made sense. I had no intentions on leaving Aaron at the moment, I only wanted him to feel the way I felt. Yea, this was tit for tat like a motherfucka, so what, sue me.

"I guess we can agree to disagree on that statement."

"I guess so, because you'll never agree to me being right." She laughed, and I joined in with her.

"You don't have to say it like that. I thank you for your advice though. I'm gonna give you a call tomorrow to let you know how everything went."

"You do that. I'll talk to you later about leaving me behind for your new friends."

"Ooh, you so shady. You know I love you the most." I never got fed into her throwing little digs she took at me being friends with Tracey. I knew if she really felt a way, she would let it be known.

"Yea, yea, don't forget to call me. And remember what I said about making that decision." I hung up the phone, and turned the music on.

Letting Tracey's words sink in, she gave me something to think about. I'd been doing the song, and dance with Aaron for long enough, and I could admit that my relationship was nowhere near where I felt it needed to be, especially after being together for so long. The love was there of course, but the like was missing. I didn't like Aaron the way I did before .

Pulling my car into Tracey, and Micah's driveway, I parked. Getting out, I went to grab my bags from the back. As if she could smell me, Eniko came running outside in her robe, and flip flops.

"Aunty Manda," she called out to me.

"Hey beautiful girl. Here, grab this for me." I handed her a bag, closed my trunk, and followed her inside the house.

"Where's everybody?"

"Daddy is in his man cave with the baby, and uncle Kaiser, and Kelly is upstairs getting ready." I rolled my eyes hearing that Kaiser was here. I wasn't over what happened back at the store yet, so I didn't want to see him.

"Alright, thank you boo. Who's watching you tonight?"

"I told daddy I can watch myself, but he wasn't hearing it, so Kelly's mom is coming over."

I laughed at her talking about watching herself. "I think that's a good idea." Kissing her forehead, she ran off, and I headed upstairs to see how far Kelly was into getting herself together.

Knocking on the bedroom door twice, she called out for me to come in.

"Hey, boo," she greeted me with a big smile on her face. One thing about Kelly was she always had a smile on her face that lit up a room. She was so easy to get along with.

"Heyy, you better push through in them Givenchy thangs, and let the girls have it." I complimented her shoes while snapping my fingers.

She laughed, and kicked her heel up to show the Swarovski detailing. "You know I do what I can." The shoes paired well with the wrap around skirt she had on, and the mesh bodysuit. "So it looks like you're kind of giving Kaiser a chance. What brought on the change of heart?"

Kelly knew that I had a man, but I hadn't spoken to her in depth about where we were in the relationship. She never asked, and I was happy about it because I didn't want to have to make anything up.

"No change of heart, I'm just going out for the free meal." I chuckled, and so did she.

"You ain't no good, and you a bold face lie. Forreal tho, Amanda, Kaiser really likes you. I hope I'm not overstepping when I say this, but where does he fit in in your relationship?"

And there it was, the relationship talk. Before I could answer, Micah walked in the door with MJ who was crying.

"What y'all do to my baby?" She asked, reaching for him.

"We ain't do nothing. He's been sleeping the whole time, and just woke up wildin'. Wassup, Manda." He gave Kelly the baby, and gave me half a hug. "You know that nigga Kaiser smelled you on the walk in. He down there asking for you."

I smirked thinking about what he may have been saying about me. "He can see me once I'm dressed, and ready to go. Let me go head, and get to it." As I went to walk out of the room, I doubled back. "Oh, and don't be tryna use these few minutes that I'm getting dressed as time to get nasty. I know how y'all do."

"Man, this my crib. If I wanna tear her ass up in the driveway I will," Micah let me know.

"Really, Micah?" Kelly squealed. "Don't listen to him Amanda. I left you a towel, and wash cloth in the guest bathroom." Laughing, I thanked her and closed the door.

In the guest bathroom, I turned the shower, and stripped out of my clothes. Thinking about Kelly's outfit, I felt like I was gonna be underdressed to the dinner, but still cute. Satisfied with the temperature of the water, I stepped inside. The heat of the water made the bathroom fog up, oddly bringing me to think about how the fog mirrored my relationship, or whatever it was that I was in at the moment. Was I using Kaiser as a distraction from my problems, or was I on my way to accepting that the relationship with Aaron had run its course? While I figured it out, I planned to live life, and see where the chips fell.

11

KAISER

"You got a little crying ass baby. I hope when Amanda give my seed, he be a chill lil' nigga like his pops," I said to Micah as he walked back into the man cave.

"Nigga, shut up," he chuckled. "He only cried like that because I went to put him in your arms. Ya aura ain't right." He kept laughing, and went over to the bar to pick up his drink.

"Man, please, babies love me. How long before we leave outta here?"

"Shouldn't be too much longer. Amanda went to jump in the shower. And how she gon' give you a baby when she got a man, bro? You really be forgetting that fact."

"Nah, nigga, I didn't forget. I just don't give a fuck. I don't know how many times I gotta tell y'all that." I shook my head at him, and threw back the last of my D'usse.

I would respect Amanda's relationship if I knew the nigga was treating her right, but he wasn't. And no, she didn't come right out, and tell me that, but she didn't have to. I'd known her for as long as I'd known Tracey, and I picked up on the change in her. She put on a front for everyone else, including her cousin, but I was in tune with her.

"Man, I don't know what's up with they relationship, but Aaron seem like a cool dude. I'm rooting for you all day tho bro. You can't help who you fall in love with."

"Right. I hope you rooting for me with bail money if that nigga try to put up a fight for her too. I'm popping that nigga soon as he get outta pocket, end of story."

"Boy, you a loose cannon."

"So I heard. Do you mind if I go up, and check on her progress?" I rubbed my hands together, and a sneaky smile crept up on my face.

"Go head man. And keep it down." I waved him off, and headed upstairs.

I knew he'd told her that I was here, and she was playing like she ain't wanna see a nigga. As I took the steps, I ran into Eniko coming down.

"Aunty Manda is in the guest room getting dressed," she said, with her face buried in her phone, not even bothering to look at me. There was no secret how I felt about Amanda, even she knew it.

"Thanks, lil' one." I took a right at the steps, and knocked on the door.

"Who is it?"

"Ya husband," I answered.

"I'm getting dressed, Kaiser!" She shouted, and I smiled. She knew what was up. She didn't say I couldn't come in, so I ceased the opportunity, and opened the door. "Didn't I just tell you that I was getting dressed." She had a scowl on her face, but my focus was on her standing before me in her panties and bra.

She had on some lingerie type shit. Some mesh kind of material covered the pussy part, giving me a good view of her bald mound. I didn't bother trying to hide the fact that I was openly staring. Licking my lips, my eyes traveled back up to her face.

"You need help?"

"No, I don't, and you are invading my privacy."

"I was just coming to check on you. We have reservations, we don't wanna be late."

"Okay, the longer you stand here, the longer it'll take me to get dressed," she responded with an attitude.

"Who made you mad?"

"Nobody." Picking up a pair of tights from the bed, I watched as she slid them up each leg, and did two hops to pull them over her ample ass. Before she could slide her shirt over her head, I walked over, and stopped in front of her. "Move, Kaiser." She tried pushing me away from her, but I stood firm.

"I'll leave once you tell me what's wrong. You can't be sitting up in the restaurant with hostility towards me, and I don't know why."

"I ran into one of your little whores at Saks today," she let out.

"Which one? Don't none of my whores work at Saks." I laughed, but her face stayed stoic. "My bad. Who you talking about?"

"The chick you were with at Karma's, the night me, Kelly, and D were out."

I knew who she was talking about, but didn't bother mentioning a name. "Okay, did she do or say something out of pocket?"

"Not directly to me of course, but about me to the busted chick she was with. I had to check her wack ass too. I don't wanna have to do that every time I run into someone you've run into. And you know what I mean by that too."

"Awww, my baby feeling a type of way. Come here girl, let me love up on you." I grabbed at her hand, and pulled her into my arms.

"Get off me, boy." She pushed me back, and I laughed.

"You want me to cut these bitches off, no problem, bae."

"That's not what I said. I don't want you doing nothing on the account of me. We're not together."

"Yet, but I'ma let you have that. I'll be waiting downstairs for you." I didn't give her a chance to respond before leaving the room, and closing the door behind me. Amanda knew what it was no matter how many times she told herself what it wasn't.

We decided to take two cars, so Amanda had to ride with me. I don't know what kind of talk her and Kelly had before coming downstairs, but I appreciated it because she was friendlier on the drive to the restaurant. Amanda looked bad as fuck in a pair of latex pants, a bandeau top with a three quarter blazer over it, and a pair of YSL pumps that made her taller than what she was. Where she usually stopped at my shoulder, the extra boost in the heels made her eye level with me.

"You look good ma," I complimented as we drove.

"Thank you, Kaiser. You look good too."

"You know a nigga had to put on for you." I winked, and she laughed. "How'd everything coming along with your new shop?" She gave me a shocked look, and I didn't understand why. "What's with the look?"

"Nothing, I'm just surprised that you're asking about my business. I had no clue that you knew about it."

"You would be surprised at what I know."

"It's moving. I found a space to rent, now I'm on to decorating. It's really exciting, kind of like birthing a baby. Thank you for asking."

"Not a problem. I think it's dope that you're going into business for yourself. Being your own boss is the best thing you can do."

"You're right about that," she agreed.

I parked my car on the corner of where the restaurant was, and went around to the passenger side to let her out. She smiled as she stepped out of the car.

"This is officially our second date, you know that right?"

"You are crazy. This is our second outing together. I wouldn't call it a date."

"You just love playing hard to get." I put my hand on her lower back, allowing her to walk in front of me. "We have reservations under Micah," I said to the waitress. We were escorted to our table where Micah, and Kelly were already seated.

"Y'all got here fast," Amanda said as she took her seat.

"Only a couple minutes ago. You know Micah drive like he's an extra on Fast & Furious," Kelly clowned.

"That's only when you do that thing while I'm driving," Micah said with no shame. I dapped him up while Kelly slapped his arm.

"If you don't shut up," she chastised.

"Right, ion wanna know all that," Amanda added while giggling.

I fucked with Micah, and Kelly's relationship. The dynamic was cool. You could tell by the way they dealt with each other that they were considerate of the others feelings. I knew that if Amanda gave me a chance that I'd have something real like that with her. Looking over at her, her face was twisted up as she typed aggressively on her phone. I could see frustration mounting all over her face.

"Excuse me, y'all, I have to take this call," she announced, getting up quickly, and walking off. I watched her, and shook my head. Only that clown ass nigga Aaron could have her so bothered.

"I'm telling you now Kaiser, in order to win her over, you are gonna have to love harder than you ever loved before. Listen, and be very attentive," Kelly advised me.

"You basically telling him to be like me," Micah joked.

"Can't nobody be you, baby." She kissed his lips, and this nigga blushed.

"What a way to make this moment about y'all. Y'all are something else." They both laughed, and Amanda made her way back to the table. Her facial expression hadn't changed.

"I'm sorry to cut out on y'all, but I gotta handle something at home," she said while picking up her purse.

"Say the word and I'll end that nigga," I assured her.

"Right now is not the time to be playing, Kaiser," she snapped.

"When have you known me to play about you?" I questioned. I'd tear some shit up behind her.

"Anyway, Kelly I'm gonna call you tomorrow." She walked over to where Kelly, and Micah were sitting, and hugged the both of them.

"I'd feel better if you called me as soon as you got home," Kelly reasoned.

"Okay, no problem. Let me get out here before this Uber leaves me."

"Why you call an Uber when I'm right here, and your car at they crib?"

"I'll get it tomorrow, Kaiser. And I'll call you tomorrow as well. Sorry if I ruined dinner." She bent down, and kissed my cheek. A nigga got all warm inside.

I decided not to go after her tonight. I needed to give Amanda space to get her house in order. By no means was I falling back, but I didn't want to pressure her either.

"Now I gotta sit here and watch y'all two be all lovey dovey."

"Nigga, you can leave, and let me have this solo dinner with my woman," Micah let out, and I chuckled.

"And miss out on the free meal, hell na. Go head and call the waitress, and let her know I'm ready to order the steak, and lobster."

DINNER WITH KELLY, and Micah was cool. Seeing that it was only ten, I wasn't ready to turn in yet, so I headed to Karma's lounge. Amanda kept to her word, and texted me once she was home, and also apologized again about having to leave abruptly. She didn't have to apologize to me, I just wanted to know that she was good. She let me know that she was fine, and again, she had to handle some things.

Pulling up to Karma's, the front was packed with cars, and the line was crazy long. The music could be heard from the street. I decided to park in the back at the employee entrance. Seeing an empty spot next to Karma's Maybach, I parked there. Getting out of the car, I gave the bouncer that stood guard a head nod, and he opened the door to let me in. I went straight for the bar to get a bottle of water. I wasn't in the mood to drink after I threw back two glasses of D'usse at the restaurant.

"Wassup, Raynell," I spoke to the bartender as she manned the bar.

"Hey, Kaiser. Make the order quick baby because these motherfuckas in here is rowdy tonight." She busied herself, pouring and serving drinks while she spoke to me.

"Just toss me a bottle of water. Karma here?"

"Ain't he always?" She answered with a chuckle. "You need to find your brother a girlfriend. In all of the jobs I've held, I've never seen any owners in their place of business more than Karma." She tossed me a water, and I laughed.

Karma lived at the club. Every now and then he would dibble and dabble in our day to day operations, but for the most part he was here.

"It's gonna be a while before that shit happen, ma. I'ma send somebody over to help you with the bar."

"You better not send nobody over here, Kaiser. You know this is what I do baby. Have a goodnight." She winked at me, and went back to doing her job.

Moving through the club, I headed to the vip entrance. Seeing a familiar bouncer, I nodded my head and he opened the door, letting me up. As always, when I got upstairs, Karma was standing at the window, overlooking the club.

"Do you ever go home?"

"Yea, when we close. What you doing here?" I dapped him up, and stood next to him.

"I had dinner with Micah and Kelly tonight."

"Oh, you third wheeling it now?" He laughed and I gave him the finger.

"I ain't into that lame shit. I was there with Amanda, but she had to breeze before we were able to order."

"Her real man must've summoned her home."

"I would be offended if I didn't know how she really felt."

"And how is that bro?" We both sat down, and he reached for his drink.

"Amanda know where she belongs. She stay with that nigga because she's scared of starting over. See, I've thought about this shit from all angels already bro. My time is coming, and I'ma put a ring on it as soon as it happens."

"Whoa, a ring? Date the girl first, nigga."

"What you think we doing now, Karma?" I asked seriously. He bust out laughing, and waved me off.

"I ain't even fucking witchu man."

I shrugged my shoulders, and went to people watching. As I looked into the sea of people, my eyes zoomed in on one of the private sections. *Well I'll be damned*, I said to myself. My eyes weren't playing tricks on me. I was watching Amanda's dude hugged up with another nigga. This wasn't no brotherly hug either.

"Get the fuck outta here," I said out loud.

"What happened?" Karma asked, sitting up in his seat.

"Look at this shit." I pointed out the window, in the direction of the section that Aaron was sitting in.

"What am I looking at bro? There's a big ass crowd of people down there."

"To your far left, bro that's Amanda's boy over there cupcaking it with another nigga." Karma didn't say anything at first. I'm sure it was because he was just as shocked as me.

"Nah, that nigga is undercover?"

"It looks that way," I responded while watching him like a hawk. They were hugged up, and real familiar with each other. That shit had me sick to my stomach. I had nothing against the gays at all. I respected the community as long as they respected me. What I had a problem with was these down low mother-fuckas. Pulling out my phone, I went to my camera and made sure to zoom in on the couple before snapping a picture.

"What you gon' do with that, show it to Manda?"

"That nigga gon' end up telling on hisself. This is just insur-ance." Putting my phone away, I sat back down and took a sip of my water. I didn't know how this was gonna play out, but I hoped for Amanda's sake that she wasn't still fucking this clown.

12

DOMINIQUE

I had been pacing the floor in my room for the last twenty minutes, trying to figure out what I was gonna wear tonight for this dinner with Karma. Even with his reminder about the dinner earlier in the week, I still wasn't ready; mentally at least. I had been on some dates in the past year, so that wasn't the reason for my nervousness. I was more so nervous about being on a date with Karma. Karma's presence commanded any room he was in, much like mine from a female stand point. He had an air of confidence, and the ability to speak to me on a level that did something to my body.

Stopping mid-walk, I sat down on the edge of my bed. Taking a deep breath, I picked up my phone and dialed Amanda's number. I could've called Kelly, but I didn't like calling on her too much these days. Not because of anything bad, but because she had family to deal with that consisted of two kids, and a fiancé. She didn't need to be bothered with my nonsense. I would be sure to fill her in on the date tomorrow at work though.

"Hey, girl. What you up to?" She answered.

"Girl, I'm so glad you picked up. Are you busy?"

"Nope."

"Okay, I'm about to Facetime you." I selected the option to Facetime on my phone, and she picked up.

"Ooh, your face is beat honey. Where you stepping out to?"

"I'm supposed to be going out to dinner with Karma." Her face lit up before I could finish talking. "Uh, uh, don't go marrying us off in your head just yet. But I do have butterflies girl."

"That's because you like him a lil' bit." She motioned with her fingers, making me laugh.

"I don't really know him like that yet, Amanda. I've only been in the same room with him a handful of times, and those times have been around the office. We don't have what you and Kaiser have." I snuck the last part in there, seeing if she'd take the bait. I noticed how they interacted with each other, and personally felt that they would make a beautiful couple.

"Aht, aht, me and Kaiser don't have anything."

"Ooh, I know if he heard you saying that he would say otherwise."

"Anyway," she playfully rolled her eyes. "What you wearing tonight?"

"I don't wanna do too much, so I was thinking boyfriend jeans, a bodysuit and a good shoe. Oh, and my .380. You can never be too careful."

"So you going full on bad bitch, I like it." We both laughed, and talked for a few more moments before she gave me encouraging words and we hung up. I felt better after talking to her, and that was needed. Checking the time again, I had about an hour to get dressed. I could work with that. My makeup was done, so I was already halfway to being ready.

Sliding into my Fenty panty and bra set, I checked myself out in the mirror. I looked so damn good, I could stay home and do my own self. Wanting to be ready a couple minutes before time,

I quickly got dressed and was pleased with my outfit choice. We agreed that Karma would pick me up from my place, and we'd make our way to the restaurant together. He still hadn't told me where we were going. I was okay with that because I liked surprises.

Adding another coat of lip gloss to my lips, I touched up my baby hairs. The braids that Amanda had put in my head were still holding up, and I was thankful. I decided to wrap the braids up in a bun to keep from having to pull them out of my face. Feeling good about my look, I grabbed a light jacket from the closet, and my Dior purse. Picking up my phone, I noticed that I'd missed a text from Karma. I hoped that he wasn't cancelling the plans after I'd gotten all cute. That would surely piss me off. Opening my phone, I read the message.

Karma: Hey, beautiful. I know we agreed that we'd drive our own cars to the restaurant, but I didn't want you to have to worry about that. I took the liberty of having a driver sent to you. When you go outside, look for a Navy blue Bentley truck. See you soon, ma.

My face lit up while reading the text. The fact that he even thought to have a driver set up for me showed the caliber of dude I was about to be entertaining. Like Micah, Kaiser did things on a grand scale, but quiet enough not to draw attention to himself. I responded to the text as I walked out of the door.

Me: You didn't have to do that, but I appreciate it. I'm leaving my place now.

Sliding my phone into my purse, I headed for the elevator. On the ride down, I took a deep breath and put myself in the headspace where I could enjoy myself. As promised, there was a Bentley truck parked outside of my building, and a guy in a suit standing outside of it.

"Domonique?" The driver asked.

"Yes, that's me," I confirmed. He nodded his head, and

opened the door to the backseat. When I looked inside, there was a big bouquet of red roses sitting on the seat, along with a small bag from Cartier. I looked over at the driver who just shrugged his shoulders with a smile. Hopping inside, I thanked him and we pulled off.

I marveled at the roses, and opened the gift bag. Inside was a box, and a handwritten note. Going for the note first, I read it to myself.

Try not to overthink this token of my appreciation for you helping me obtain my new home, and accompanying me on this date tonight. Would you consider this corny?

I laughed out loud at the note and slid it into my purse as a keepsake. It was just too cute. By the shape of the jewelry box, I knew I was in for a treat. Opening it up, I marveled at the rose gold Love Necklace. This man was making it hard not to be interested in him. Pulling out my phone, I sent him a text to thank him.

Me: You really did not have to do all of this, but I so appreciate the thought and the fact that you thought I was worth it all.

Karma: You're worth that and then some, beautiful.

"We're here," the driver announced. I noticed that we were parked outside of Ipic theaters and became intrigued.

"Ooook," I dragged out as the driver got out to open my door.

"Walk up to the front and someone will be there to escort you in," he instructed. I picked up the flowers and my gift and headed to the entrance.

Like he said, there was a woman standing at the door waiting for me.

"Right this way." I followed behind the woman, thinking to myself how unique this whole set up was. Reaching theatre seven, she opened the doors, and it was empty with the exception of Karma who stood in the middle of the aisles.

"Thank you, Sarah," he said to the woman who smiled and walked back out the door.

"Did you rent out this whole theatre?" I asked while walking toward him.

"I did. I figured we could watch some classic flicks, and do dinner after."

I nodded my head. "This is really cool and unique. You're setting the bar really high, Mr. Karma." I put my hand into his open hand, and he guided me to my seat.

"Top tier shit only, ma. You can press the button on the side of your chair if you wanna order anything.

"I hear you big timer. So what we watching?"

"Two Can Play That Game." He smirked at me, and I bust out laughing. This was gonna be an interesting date, and I couldn't wait to see what he had in store for dinner.

"So what did you think of dinner?" He asked as he drove me back to my place.

I looked over at him and bust out laughing. "You know, when we pulled up to the Popeyes, I thought you were joking."

He laughed along with me. "Nah, I had to know if you were really gonna be down. By the way you was bussing that chicken down, I knew you were a rider."

"Oh, so you were testing me?"

"Something like that, and you passed."

"Okay, I'll let you have that because renting out the theatre was cute, and having the whole Popeyes to ourselves was cool too. You won't get a pass on the next date though." I let the last part of my statement slip, but I had such a good time, I didn't bother trying to correct myself.

"I get a second date?"

"Yep." I smiled and he smirked at me. The man was too fine.

"Do you like to travel?" He asked, randomly.

"I love traveling, I don't get to do much though because my schedule is so hectic. I love a good island."

"How you feel about going on a trip with me? You know, as a second date."

"It's a little too soon for that, don't you think?" Karma was cool and all, but a trip for the second date was kind of pushing it.

"I understand. If it makes you feel any better, Micah will be there with Kelly, and I'm sure Kaiser is looking for ways to convince Amanda to come with him." Hearing that the girls would be there made me want to say yes, but I still had to mull it over. Maybe a talk with them would convince me a little more.

"When is the trip set for, and where is the destination?"

"Columbia, and you have a week to think about it."

"Okay." We drove for another twenty minutes before we reached my building. "Thank you for a fun filled, informative night." I said to him as I reached for the handle on my door to get out.

"No problem. It was a pleasure. Here, let me get the door for you." I watched as he got out, and came to my side of the car. He held his hand out to help me out of the low seated Ferrari. I clutched my bouquet of flowers in my hand and made sure that I had a good balance in my heels.

"Shoot me a text when you get inside, so that I know you made it in safely."

"Will do." I leaned in and kissed his cheek. "Goodnight, Karma."

"Goodnight, beautiful."

I walked towards my building, and butterflies filled my stomach. I hadn't had butterflies since my first boyfriend in Highschool, who was the love of my life. You couldn't tell me that me and Tim weren't gonna be married right out of college, with a beautiful daughter named Imani. That didn't work out after I found out he cheated half of our relationship. I think that's where my trust in men started to die. No, actually, it died when I started to realize that I didn't have a father like most of the girls in my neighborhood. Anyway, it felt like Kaiser had the potential to make me believe in love again. I was interested in seeing what that would look like.

13

KARMA

After getting the message from Domonique letting me know that she made it upstairs, I drove off, en route to the club. The whole night I sat across from her at dinner, I couldn't keep my eyes off of her. Not only was she dressed to kill, but the way she carried herself said a lot about her. The whole Popeyes thing started out as a joke at first, and I'd made back up reservations at Houstons, but the fact that she went along with it made her perfect in my eyes. I half expected her to cuss my ass out, especially after telling me in not so many words that I needed to come correct when I first asked her out. It was nothing like being in the presence of a woman who was classy, but could be a little hood as well.

I hoped that she agreed to the Columbia trip because it would be good to see her let her hair down a bit more. I think the idea of having both Kelly, and Amanda there as her buffers would make her feel more at ease. As I made my way to the club, I got an incoming call from Raven. Answering the call, I placed it on speakerphone.

"What's good?"

"Aye, man, sorry to interrupt you on your day off, but we

have a problem." Her tone was even, but there was a hint of irritation in it as well.

"What kind of problem? I'm already headed that way."

"The kind that requires the owner's attention."

"Say that." I hung up the phone, and hit the gas, making the Ferrari do the numbers that it was made to do. From Domonique's crib, I got to the club in fifteen minutes flat. Pulling around back, I got out and entered through the employees entrance. It prevented me from having to walk through the sea of people and give out a bunch of wassups. Inside, I went straight for Raven's office to see if she was there. Knocking on the door, I heard her give the okay to come in.

Inside, Raven was seated behind her desk, while Trina, one of my best waitresses sat across from her. You could feel the tension in the room.

"Wassup?" I asked.

Trina whipped her head in my direction, and judging by the look on her face, she was pissed off. "Wassup is the fact that you put this bulldagger in charge, and it's not working for me," she spat. I looked over at Raven, who sat back in her chair with her hands crossed, seemingly unfazed by the name calling.

"First, let's start over by showing your manager some respect. You've been on the team long enough to know that disrespect will not be tolerated," I checked her. I wasn't gonna let her think that it was okay to talk to Raven crazy in her face or when she wasn't around. I didn't care that she'd been here longer. "Now, what's the problem?"

"The problem is, she just accused me of pocketing money, and pulled me off the floor in the middle of a busy night like I'm some child."

I looked over at Raven, whose facial expression never changed and then back at Trina. "Have you pocketed any money?" I asked.

"Are you serious right now, Karma? You know—."

I cut her off with a wave of my hand. "Listen to the question, Trina and keep in mind that we have cameras all around this club for your safety in more ways than one." I hoped that she understood the underlying message in what I was saying to her. "Have you pocketed any money?"

"No," she responded with a straight face.

"Aight. Raven, pull the cameras up for me." She turned on her Mac pc and pulled up the footage like I'd asked. "What time did you clock in tonight, and which tables did you work?" I asked Trina.

"I clocked in at nine and I worked tables nine through eleven."

"Pull the footage from nine up until the time you pulled her off the floor," I instructed and walked closer to Raven's desk so that I could see.

"Wait," Trina yelled out, "Karma, can I talk to you in private?" Her eyes started to water, confirming what I already knew by her being on the defense when I walked in.

"Nah, you had your opportunity to be honest. Here you are, clearly pocketing the money from every tab you picked up tonight. Damn, did you even think to give the house any money?" I watched as she strategically worked her tables, sticking the tab plus whatever tips she was given in her pocket.

"Karma, let me just explain."

"Notice how when someone gets caught doing some fraud shit they wanna explain. I'm not disputing that whatever you have to say isn't important, I'm just not tryna hear up because you openly lied to a nigga face. Anything you needed, you know for a fact you could've come to me, ma, but you chose this route. Usually niggas get bodied for this type of offense, but I'ma just let you go on and pack up. Leave that bread right here though." I pointed to Raven's desk and went to walk out. "After you make sure that she's out of my club, come holla at me, Raven."

To know that Trina had been stealing from the house didn't

sit well with me. She looked real comfortable on the camera which only let me know that she'd done this before. The crazy thing is, there was no way I could've missed it seeing as I'd been doing the count up until Raven took over the day to day operations. The knock on my office door pulled me from my thoughts.

"Come in," I called out and Raven entered.

"You handled that?"

"Yea. I really wanted to beat her ass though, but figured that would be unprofessional."

"How you pick up on what she was doing?"

"I watched her. She was way too willing to help tonight. You know how we usually assign the waitresses to two tables each?" I nodded my head yes. "Well, ya girl requested three tables, citing that it was busy and the guys at the table requested her. At first I didn't mind but I noticed that she wasn't going to the bar to clear her orders in the system. I pulled her off the floor, and tried to reason with her that if she kept it 100 and put the money in my hand, I'd let her go with a suspension.

"Nah, ain't no suspension when you take money out of my pockets and those employed here. Yo ass gets terminated, end of discussion. You give motherfuckas an inch, they take a mile, then I take their lives." She nodded her head catching my drift.

"Got you, but I don't anticipate us having that problem ever again," she assured me.

"Oh, I know we won't have that problem again. I'll cut a motherfucka hand off before the thought even crosses their mind. Everything else good here though?"

"Yea, business is good, you know that."

"Aight, well go head and get back to doing your thing. And I haven't gotten a chance to tell you, but I appreciate what you do around here. Don't ever let nobody come out their face to you again. Motherfuckas do it once they gon' think they can do it again."

"I appreciate that, Karma. Everybody know what it is around

here. Trina was doing all that to get under my skin and to show off in front of you. She was just wanting to suck my dick two nights ago." We both laughed and she left my office.

After what had just occurred, I decided to stay for the rest of the night until closing. I was gonna triple count the money tonight to make sure all tickets were accounted for. They didn't wanna see the reason my pops named me Karma.

I DIDN'T GET HOME until four in the morning, and couldn't get to sleep for shit. I don't know why but I found myself thinking about my mother. Although she'd never been a part of our lives, my father made it a point of letting us know where she was. He always felt it was up to us if we decided to reach out. A few years ago I had someone track down her latest address in the city. I wasn't ready to rekindle that mother/son relationship because that time had already passed.

But now I really wanted to get to know her more than anything, and find out what type of person he really was. Also what was going through her head when she decided to leave us. It was kind of uncommon for a mother to willingly leave her children if there weren't any extenuating circumstances. Supposedly that wasn't the case with my mother, Vivian. Apparently she didn't want children, and being trapped by my father with me and Kaiser didn't change her mind. Before my pops died, he told me and Kaiser to not force a relationship with her. If she wanted us, to let her form that bond, because that would mean she had grown out of being the selfish woman he knew.

So far, I'd been sticking to that, but with her heavily on my mind, I knew I needed to see her face. Getting out of bed, I redressed myself, and headed to Kaiser's crib. I knew he would be pissed about me showing up in the wee hours in the morning, but he couldn't beat me. Driving through the streets of

Manhattan in the early morning hours was real peaceful. It gave me time to think. Now that I was actively pursuing Domonique, I needed to ensure that I didn't have any mommy issues that I hadn't dealt with. I was a grown man about my shit at all times, so if I had any faults I owned up to them.

Domonique was a different caliber of woman, so I wanted to make sure that my mental was good enough to cover us both if need be. Pulling up to the high rise that Kaiser lived in, I parked on the street, and entered the building. I gave the doorman a head nod as I walked past and got on the elevator. Like me, Kaiser had given me a spare key to his place to use for emergencies. Unlike him, I only used mine for its purpose, so I rang his doorbell instead of entering his place on my own.

"Who dat?" He called out about two minutes later.

"Your brother."

"Can't be my brother. My brother would know not to come to my crib at this hour. Stop playing at my door before I let this bitch blow through this mutherfucking door." I heard two taps on the door from his side and chuckled. This guy was a real life clown. I didn't bother going back and forth with him. Sticking the key in the door, I let myself in. He stood on the other side of it with his gun at his side.

"You really need medication my nigga."

"You know I ain't got no home training. What you doing at my crib this late? Somebody fucking witchu?" He asked while closing and locking the door.

"I'ma bout to go meet up with ma in a few hours," I said with a serious expression.

"I need you to be more specific, whose ma?" He scratched his head, playing dumb.

"Our mother, fool."

"You mean your mother, and my egg donor. What you going to see her for? If you need to lay your burdens down, I'm right here."

"I'm going to see her because I have a couple questions for her, and I think you should come too." I threw the last part in there on a whim because I felt a face to face conversation with her would benefit him as well. He deserved answers just as much as I did.

"I don't need to go because I know all I need to know. She walked away from us, the end. You're more than welcome to sleep in the guest bedroom. A nigga tired as shit. I need to do some last minute shopping and convincing of Amanda to go on this trip with us next week." He went to walk off and I stopped him.

"Bro, come on. I need you to come through for me on this one. If you don't have anything to say to her, that's cool. Just come in support of me."

His face frowned up, and I was well aware that I was asking a lot of him. "You asking a lot, but I'ma go because you in here looking like you bout to cry and shit."

"Fuck you, man." I laughed and he did too. My father taught us to be there for each other no matter what, especially in the times where it pained us to do so. That's when we knew we needed each other the most.

I made my way to his guest room, and removed my sweat pants, revealing a pair of basketball shorts underneath. I was sure that the visit with my mother was gonna be both enlightening and entertaining to say the least. I never knew what to expect with my brother. I just hoped he didn't go too far. At the end of the day, she was still our mother.

THE RIDE to my mother's side of town was a silent one. She was over in a part of east New York that was still dilapidated. Urban gentrification had not made its way there yet. I had my music turned down to a low level, and Kaiser sat in the passenger seat with his head rested against the window, and his eyes closed. I knew he wasn't sleeping though. He was trying to avoid talking about the meeting. I figured it was only right that I gave him that being that I was basically dragging him with me. As I drove my phone rang, and seeing that it was Domonique calling, I connected the call.

"Beautiful, to what do I owe the pleasure."

"Just calling to say, hey. What are you up to?"

"I'm on the way to visit my mother," I answered like it was a regular occurrence for me.

"Oh, okay. I hope that goes well." Over dinner she'd asked me about my relationship with my mom, and I told her I didn't have one. She told me that a man's relationship with their mother told a lot about who they were as a man. I could agree to an extent, but it was a good thing that me and Kaiser didn't grow up to be no fuck niggas. Although I always believed that my mother's absence had possibly led to some female trust issues as far as opening our hearts and feelings to women. But now with the presence of Dominique in my life and Amanda conceivably in Kaisers. Maybe we were just in need of the right women.

"Yea, I hope so too. Did you give any thought to going on the trip?"

"I did, and I talked to Kelly this morning. I'm gonna go because I could use the break."

"That's what I'm talking about. All expenses will be paid for, and shopping on me." Kaiser looked over at me and mouthed, sucker,

"You ain't gotta treat me, baby. I'm a boss too. Just make sure that my room is lavish when I get there." I liked when she talked that boss shit. You don't meet too many women out there handling they shit. "Let me let you go, I have some work I need to get to."

"Aight, don't work too hard. I'ma hit you later on."

"Sounds good. I'd love to hear how the meet up with your

mom went. Remember to give her a chance to explain herself. You only get one mother." I knew about Dominique losing her parents at a young age so I knew this was a touchy subject for her. She had also slightly opened up about the God mother who had taken her in. It didn't seem like it was a nurturing situation because she got real emotional before cutting off the conversation.

"I hear you Mami. Have a good day." We hung up at the same time, and I put the phone down.

"So you're sponsoring shopping trips now, bro?" Kaiser clowned, now sitting up in his seat.

"Man, stay out my conversation. You need to worry about convincing Amanda to come on this trip because right now there's only five people confirmed, and none of them is Amanda."

"Oh, she coming nigga, trust me."

I parked my car in front of the bakery that my mother owned, and turned off the ignition. It was a few older crackheads hanging out in front of the small building that looked like it was about to fall in. She'd opened up the place about two years ago and it seemed to be in the wrong area. The only thing selling over this way was something to smoke or shoot up in your arm. Hearing Kaiser sigh, I put my attention on him.

"You good?"

"Yea, let's go in and get this shit over with." He went for the door handle, and stopped before getting out. "Oh, and when we get in here, don't try to speak for me. Speak for you and you only," he made clear.

I nodded my head, and stepped out of the car. At the end of the day, Kaiser was his own man, so I had no intentions of speaking on his behalf. Although the questions I wanted to ask would lead to answers for us both. Entering the place, the door chimed and I made my way to the counter.

"Good afternoon," I greeted one of the servers.

"Hi, welcome to Viv's Place. Are you selling or buying?" The older cashier responded back all perky and shit.

"Is the owner here?"

"Umm, yea, you ain't no cop are you?" The look of concern on her face was evident.

I smirked before responding. "Nah, you can tell her that Karma is here though. She'll know the name." Saying my name out loud was fitting for the moment.

As the woman went off to the back, I turned to Kaiser. His head was in his phone, not the least bit interested in what was going on. I turned back just as the woman was returning to the counter.

"You guys can follow me back here," she instructed with a wave of her hand. We followed behind her, down a hallway until we got to a door. On the door read the words, boss. I laughed inwardly.

"Come on in," my mother said from the other side of the door before her employee could knock. I nodded my head at the woman, and pushed the door open myself. "How'd you find me?"

"I've always known where you were. I never had a reason to come to you until now. You got time to talk?"

"You sound just like your damn father," she said with a smirk. She sat back in her seat, and looked past me to where Kaiser was standing. "You don't have anything to say to me, Kaiser?" He ignored her and kept his eyes on his phone. "I see you have some of your father in you as well."

"Did you know that you didn't wanna be a mother when you married our father?" I asked, getting to the reason why we were here.

"Yes I knew and your father knew also. Me and him had some real good shit going on, but he decided to become a damn muslim when he got locked up for a lil stint. Nigga came home talking about how he was a changed man and now he wanted a family. He really thought I was about to give my life up to become some muslim wife all covered up and shit. That wasn't the life I wanted for myself and since I'm guessing you want full honesty. Did your great father tell yall, he threatening to take my life, if I had an abortion? I'm sure he didn't speak on all the things he had done that let me know that wasn't an ide threat."

Kaiser snickered while I wanted to hear more.

"So it was a safety thing for you in given birth to us?"

"That, and your father promised me financial security and as you can see, he didn't keep his word. I'm hoping you both are here today to make good on that promise."

"Are you fucking serious?" Kaiser spat.

"Did you ever love our father?" I asked, totally ignoring her shaking us down for money.

"Yea, I loved Koran. He loved y'all more though, now about that money, I have a plan on how we can open up a chain of these bakeries across the city."

"Yo you really are crazy, why would we give you anything?" Kaiser asked looking strangely at her.

"Because I gave your ungrateful ass life! You think I don't know what yall do, I've kept my eye on y'all also. I know how you getting money out here and it ain't just from that damn lounge of yours." she yelled now looking at me.

She really had turned this whole meeting into something all about her. I didn't like that shit at all.

Nodding my head, I heard all I needed to hear. "That's all I needed to know. After hearing you talk, I now know that we didn't miss out on anything growing up. We had an abundance of love around us, our father made sure of it. You be cool, Vivian." I nodded my head towards Kaiser, letting him know that I was ready to go.

"What about the investment baby, she asked in a motherly tone," as I opened the door. I went to respond, but Kaiser did instead.

"I'm going to tell you the same thing my father told you many years ago, you really are sorry. I'm glad you left or we would have been some simp niggas out here begging for love and attention from a woman who was incapable of giving it to us. I ain't even mad at you forreal. Because of you, I'm gonna make sure I love on my woman a little harder, so that when she brings our little one into the world she'll have enough love to go around and then some." With that, we walked out, and made our way back to the car.

"Thanks for holding it down back there," I said to him and put my fist up to him. He tapped it twice.

"You know I'll go to hell witchu, bro. This wasn't far from it."

I chuckled, and so did he. "Yo, what woman were you talking about?" I couldn't help but to fuck with him.

"Man, you just had to fuck up the moment. Drive me back home, dawg."

Still chuckling, I pulled out. Now that I had the answers I needed from my mother, I could confirm that her leaving had nothing to do with us, and everything to do with her. I could move on with a clear conscience that she made her choice and had made peace with it. Now I could do the same.

14

AMANDA

I watched Aaron from my bed as he packed his suitcase for one of his business trips. Unlike the previous times, I wasn't eyeing everything he put in the bag. In fact, I was counting down the minutes until he left. Shit was off between us, and the dry sex we had last night solidified that. When he called my phone last night while I was out to dinner, questioning where I was and who I was with, I actually felt guilty that I was out smiling in Kaiser's face. Granted, I'd found those messages in his phone, but a part of me still wanted to work it out. I couldn't do that if I was out entertaining Kaiser.

I took an Uber home and when I walked through the door, to say I was shocked was an understatement. He had rose petals on the floor and candles lit all around our living room. It was so beautiful I had to coach myself not to cry. It was a good thing that I didn't get a chance to eat back at the restaurant because he had a whole spread of food laid out. In that moment, I put everything behind me, and focused on the Aaron before me. It was the romantic Aaron that I knew and loved.

We ate, and talked about the things that could help get our relationship back on track. It felt good to be in that moment with him. Everything was going well until he touched me. When his hands touched my body I didn't get that tingling sensation that I once had if his finger even grazed my shoulder. I waited for it to come during sex, and again, nothing. What was even crazier was him wanting to only put me in the doggystyle position. Now, don't get me wrong, I was all for the face down, ass up activity.

There was something about the way he was doing it though. I couldn't put my finger on it. I just knew that I didn't like it. It wasn't familiar to me, so I faked an orgasm to get him off of me. I even played sleep so that he wouldn't try to go another round. Me fake sleeping only worked in his favor because he snuck out of the house in the middle of the night, and didn't return until about three hours ago. I was still fake sleep when he came back up until now.

"How long will you be gone for this time?" I played the role as if I really cared.

"About a week. I just got some new shit in, and it's in high demand." As he continued to pack, I made a mental note that it looked like more than a week worth of clothes.

"Okay," I simply replied. Getting out of bed, I picked up my phone, and I went to grab my robe from the back of the bedroom door when he grabbed me by my waist from behind. Again, there was no tingling sensation. I held in my sigh of disdain and allowed him to hold me.

"I feel like we reconnected last night." I wanted to say, nigga please, but I held it in. "When I get back, we're going on vacation. It's been a while since we got away together."

"Sounds good. Ohh, I gotta pee," I lied to get him off of me. Wiggling out of his embrace, I headed for the bathroom, making sure to lock the door behind me after I closed it. Turning on the water for a shower, I let it run while I sat on my toilet checking the messages I missed. Seeing two messages from Kaiser, I went to check those first.

K: Aye, I saw this on tv and it made me think of us.

Tapping the screen to download the image he'd sent, I laughed out loud when it came up. It was a picture of a couple at the alter. Why a couple getting married would make him think about he and I, I had no clue, but it was cute. That message was from earlier this morning. Clicking out of the picture, I went to the latest message he'd sent.

K: We going on vacation next week. It's a couples vacation too, so when we out there, you don't have to pretend. We can really be together like I know you want to.

Again, I snickered. I swear this guy had a couple of screws loose. I went to respond to the text when Aaron knocked at the door.

"Alright, babe, I'm out. I'll call you once I land in Atlanta." This was the first time I heard that Atlanta was his destination. No longer caring enough to dwell on it, I bid him farewell.

"Okay, have a safe trip, love ya."

"Love you too." I waited a little before turning off the water and exiting the bathroom. Checking to make sure that he'd left, I dialed Kelly's number.

"Hey, girl, what's going on?" She answered on the second ring.

"Hey, boo. I wanted to reach out and apologize again for leaving dinner last night."

"Oh, you good. Yo boo was sad that he had to watch Micah steal kisses from me all night though."

I giggled, thinking about all the shit talking Kaiser probably did while I was gone. "Tuh, had I known my night was gonna go the way it did when I came home, I would've stayed."

"Oooh, you wanna talk about it?"

"Maybe another time. Tell me about this couple's trip that Kaiser is talking about." I changed the subject because the last thing I wanted to talk about was Aaron's performance last night.

"Damn, he didn't even give me a chance to talk to you like I told him I would. Micah is going on a business trip and since

I've never been out of the country, he decided to make it a trip for me too. The guys are coming too, so we figured we'd make it a gangcation. Please tell me you're gonna be able to make it. Kaiser won't let us hear the end of it if you didn't come."

"Us? Domonique already agreed?"

"Yep. It'll be fun. Think about it, it'll be your last vacation before you dive into your business. You're gonna be so busy with that, that you won't know which way is up and which way is down." I nodded my head, knowing she was right. Aaron had said he'd be back in a week but with him being so unpredictable lately, I wouldn't hold my breath.

"Alright, I'll come under one condition."

"Yayy, what?"

"You have to make sure I don't slip up and sleep with Kaiser." She bust out laughing on the other end of the phone and I didn't see what was so funny. I was deadass serious.

"I don't have anything to do with that. You grown and on your own boo."

"Come on Kelly, please. I can see my ass up in the air on a beach already. You have to watch me."

"Amanda," she called out my name like a school teacher, "whatever you don't want to happen, won't happen. Keep in mind though, what's meant to be, will be."

"Was that supposed to be encouraging?"

"Yes, did it work?"

"No."

"Oh, well, good luck and pack light because we'll be shopping there."

"Okayyy," I dragged. "I'll talk to you later. I gotta shower and head down to the building to go over some stuff with the contractors. Domonique is meeting me there."

"Alright, boo, I'll talk to you." She hung up and I set my phone down on my bed. I knew this trip was gonna be a big eye opener for me.

PULLING up in front of the building that would house my dream in just a month, I got butterflies. It wasn't my nerves either. It was because I was actually stepping out on faith and making this thing happen for myself. I'd prayed for this with my mother and by myself on many nights, and it was coming to life right before my eyes. Just as I thought of my mother, her name flashed across my screen.

"What's going on, Queen?" I spoke into the phone once it connected.

"Hey, baby, I was just thinking about you so I thought I'd give you a ring. What you up to?" I decided to Facetime her to show her where I was. "Oh, you wanted to see my beautiful face this morning huh, daughter." I laughed once her face came into view. My mother was so beautiful and regal. It was like the sun was shining wherever she was.

"That and I wanted to show you this." I flipped the camera so that she could see the building. "It's happening, ma."

"Yes it is, baby." She clapped her hands with a big smile on her face. "I know I tell you all the time but it wouldn't hurt for you to hear it again. I am so proud of you, Amanda. You waited your turn and now God is making it happen for you. The fact that you were patient is a plus."

"Thank you, mommy. You know I appreciate your love, and guidance through this process."

"You know I got ya back, always. How's everything with you and Aaron?" I turned the camera back around to face me and let out a long sigh.

"It's not going, ma. I really think it's over." Admitting that for the first time out loud didn't cause aching in my heart like I thought it would. My mother and I were really close, so she knew all about the last few months of my woes with Aaron. "As you know, things have been off for a while and at this point, I know for sure that I'm carrying most of the emotional load of the relationship."

"And that's something I don't wanna hear. You know what I went through with your father the last few years of us being together. I wouldn't wish that kind of mental confusion on anyone." I nodded my head, knowing exactly what she was talking about. I watched my father completely break my mother down mentally.

The crazy thing is, he wasn't physically or verbally abusive, but he did have a way with his words. He led my mother on for the most part, making the outside world think that he was a devoted husband, all the while he had a stable of side chicks that catered different needs for him. Seeing that first hand, I lost all respect for him, and hadn't spoken not one word to him since he left us. It was the best decision he could've ever made on behalf of both me and my mother.

"Yea, I remember. That's why I'm going away next week to clear my head, and when I come back, I know I have some decisions to make."

"Well, okay, miss girl." She snapped her fingers in the camera. "Where you going and who you going with?"

"You know what's crazy, I don't even know where the destination is. All I know is that I agreed to go on a couples vacay with a couple, a pair that's getting to know each other, and Kaiser." I giggled thinking how crazy that sounded.

"Umm hmm, Kaiser huh. I see you, boo. You finally giving that man a chance. You might as well because he don't stop for nothing. His persistence alone makes me okay with him being my possible son in law." She smirked and winked her eye at me.

"Ma, let me let you go before you start really being in my business. And for the record, I'm not giving Kaiser a chance. Remember, I still have stuff to sort out at home," I made clear.

"Hmm, not convincing enough for me, baby. You have a good time though, and if you have time, come see me before you go. If not, I'll see you when you get back. I love you and be safe."

"I love you too, Queen." We hung up the phone, and I laughed out loud. Just like she knew about Aaron, she knew about Kaiser pursuing me. I actually told her about him the first day I met him while crying about Aaron in Micah's bathroom.

From jump, she liked how he approached me, and that moment had been etched in her mind since then. Shaking my head, I slipped my phone into my purse, and got out of the car. Locking my doors, I noticed that Domonique's all white Range Rover was parked across the street. I should've known that she would beat me here. The girl was a stickler about time. Entering the building, the contractor and his crew were busy at work. Giving everyone warm hellos, I walked over to where Domonique stood off in the corner, on her phone.

"Send over the paperwork, Allison and I'll get it done today. Okay, talk to you later." She ended her call and gave me a hug and kiss on the cheek. "Hey, mamas. You're about three minutes late, but I'ma let you slide cause you my girl."

"I am not late. I was outside on the phone with my mother."

"Do you have proof of that?" She asked with a grin on her face.

"Yep." I went to pull out my phone, and she tapped my hand.

"Girl, stop playing.," she giggled. "What do you think about the place so far?"

I looked around, and nodded my head in approval. "They're making a lot of progress. The way it's going, I'll definitely be able to open up shop by next month. When we come back from vacation, I'm gonna jump right into getting the interior decorating done. Everything is already ordered."

"Yess, you're coming on the trip too." She held her hand up for a five, and I gave her one.

"Yea, Kaiser texted me about it, and I called to confirm with

Kelly this morning. Do you know where we going? I didn't get a chance to ask her."

"Columbia, baby." She started to whine her hips, making me laugh.

"Well, okay. I've never been there but I'm excited to go. Speaking of Kaiser, I never texted him back." I pulled out my phone to text while Domonique snickered. "What you over there snickering for?"

"Because I know this trip is gonna give you all the answers you need and further solidify your relationship with Kaiser." I didn't bother responding because no matter what I said, she along with the other people in my life were gonna ignore me when I said I was cool on Kaiser. Shit, he even ignored me when I told him.

"Anyway, how'd the date go with Karma?"

She blushed, and her eyes fluttered before she spoke. "The date was really cute. He rented out the theatre for us and girl, guess where he took me for dinner?" She put her hand up to her mouth and giggled.

"Where?" I asked, skeptical.

"Girl, Popeyes. He rented out the Popeyes joint so we could eat."

"Nu, uh." I bust out laughing, making the workers turn and look at us. "Ooh, sorry guys. Come on, let's go outside." I pulled her by her arm, and once we made it back outside I laughed some more. "Popeyes, Dom, really?"

"Amanda, I swear to you. When we pulled up, my face dropped like that girl from Flavor of Love when he took her to that KFC. I said, I know he is not serious, but he was and I went with it. The chicken was fried to perfection." I doubled over, laughing because that was something that Kaiser would do. I didn't expect it from Karma.

"Well, at least you had a good time. When's the second date?"

"According to him, Columbia is the second date."

"Now that's some boss shit."

"It takes a boss to recognize something like that." We slapped fives and laughed. "I'm real excited about going now that it's gonna be me, you, and Kelly. We about to be lit in Columbia."

"You damn right, and I'm leaving all my bullshit right here in New York. I'm gonna let my hair down, and do whatever I feel is right."

"I sure hope that includes letting Kaiser break that back!"

"You know what, you a mess." I playfully pushed her. I had no intentions on having sex with anyone other than myself on this trip. I planned to chant that to myself whenever Kaiser got too close to me. This was gonna be one for the books.

15

KAISER

In less than 24 hours, Amanda and I would be going on our first trip together. I had some shit lined up for her that was gonna leave a lasting impression long after we landed back in NY. This week, I kinda fell back from contacting her so much, so that she could mentally prepare for the experience she was sure to have on this trip. I was prepared to do a lot of persuading to get her to agree to the trip. I was surprised to get a text from her saying that she would see me in Columbia. I was confused as to why she was telling me as if we weren't leaving together, but I brushed it off.

Initially this trip was for business and a little pleasure now that the ladies were confirmed, and after the visit with my egg donor, I needed the getaway. It was mind boggling to me that after all these years Karma wanted to reach out to her for answers to questions I felt were trivial now. When we got there, however, I understood. Soon as I stepped into her presence, my chest got tight. I was filled with a bunch of emotions that I didn't know were there. Better yet, I'd long ago tucked them away.

Hearing her talk nonchalantly about the decisions she made, I knew right then and there that I couldn't even entertain the thought of developing some kind of relationship with her. Vivian was selfish and I couldn't coexist with her type. When we left, I was glad that I had come to support my brother, and any ill feelings I had, I left them right there with her. I hoped that the trip would further put a lid on those feelings of emptiness when it came to not having a mother figure. A tap on my window pulled me from my thoughts. Looking up, I saw one of the runners crouched down, peeking inside.

"Back the fuck up," I barked, making him jump. Unlocking the door, I stepped out of the car and he stepped back. "Fuck is wrong witchu, knocking on my glass like that?"

"My bad, Kaiser."

"Yea, your bad. Since when you do that shit? Don't I come in the trap and get what I need?"

"Yea, my fault." His voice was shaky but he made sure not to show fear on his face. It was a good thing too because I would've had to fire his ass quick. I couldn't afford scary niggas on the team. Heading inside the building, I took the steps to the third floor and did my signature knock on apartment 3F.

"Who dat?" Someone called out.

"Kaiser." I heard the locks pop quickly and the door opened.

"What's good, Kaiser," one of the young bulls greeted and I responded with a head nod.

Since I'd taken Jeff off his post a while ago, I had one of our seasoned lieutenants, Kenny on money count. Walking into the apartment, I noticed that the place was empty with the exception of the person watching the door, and the person in the room who stood as guard for Kenny. He sat at a table, counting the money while a shotgun lay on the table beside me. This was the type of shit I liked to see. Niggas was on they post and ready for whatever.

"What's the word boss man," Kenny spoke with his fist out. I connected his with mine and took a seat across from him.

"You tell me. What that count looking like?"

"Always good, you already know how I'm coming." He wrapped a rubber band around the last stack of cash, and threw it in the duffle bag on the table before pushing it towards me along with the money counter.

No matter how cool he may have thought we were, I was always going to check the count. After thirty minutes of counting each rubber band wrapped stack and ensuring it matched the product moved in the last week, everything matched up. Not one for small talk with the workers, I dapped Kenny up and made my way out the door. Back in my car, I headed to secure the money in the safe. As I drove, my phone rang with a call from Ariane. I wasn't sure of the reason for her call, seeing as I'd stopped fucking with her.

Remembering the shit she pulled when she ran into Amanda at Saks, I ignored the call. I didn't wanna give her any reason to think it was like that with us anymore. After dropping off the money bag, I headed straight home to finish packing for the trip and then a nap. Although I planned to sleep on the plane, a power nap beforehand would do me justice.

"NIGGA, WHERE YOU AT?" Karma yelled into my ear, waking me from a peaceful nap.

"I was on a beach somewhere digging Amanda's guts out from the back, but you fucked that up." Sitting up, I shifted my hard on and sucked my teeth.

"Man, I ain't need to hear all that. You're supposed to be over here at Micah house. We gotta have a quick meeting before the ladies get here and we head out."

"Damn, I forgot all about that. Aight, lemme jump in the shower and I'll be there in a few."

"Don't take all day."

"Yea, yea." I hung up on him and threw my phone down on

the bed. Heading to the bathroom, I hopped in the shower. I was already late so there was no need in rushing. I took my normal fifteen minute shower, and got out.

Getting dressed, I grabbed the suitcase that held all of my belongings, my passport, and left out of the house. Hopping in my car, I decided to call Amanda to see what she was up to. She answered on the first ring.

"Yes, Kaiser."

"Damn, I'm getting on your nerves already?"

She chuckled. "No, wassup."

"Oh, aight. I was just calling to check on you."

"Check on me to see if I'm packed and ready to go, or checking on me just to see what I'm doing?"

"Shit, a little bit of both."

"Right now, I'm picking up some last minute things before heading over to Micah and Kelly's house."

"Sounds good, make sure you stop by one of those lingerie stores and get some sexy shit to put on."

"For who?"She responded and I could hear the smile in her voice.

"You know who. I ain't even gonna play games with you on this phone girl."

"Yea, okay." She snickered a little. "I have some rules for you on this trip."

"Rules?"

"Yes, rules. I need you to remember that we are not a couple."

"Yet."

"What?"

"We're not a couple, yet. Keep going."

"Anyway, we're not a couple. You need to keep your hands to yourself and mind your words."

"Mind my words? What are we going on a sixth grade field trip or something?"

"Kaiser! I'm serious. I'm going on this trip to have a good time and sort some things out about my relationship, not to fool around with you." She spat those words like exploring things with me would be such a bad idea. Amanda was making it hard not to just tell her what a fuck nigga her man was, but I kept quiet. I was gonna change the plans I already had set once we got to Columbia. She needed time, and I was starting to feel like I was forcing her to fuck with me, and I wasn't feeling that at all. Especially after that conversation with my egg donor Vivian. She had shown me what trying to make someone be something they didn't desire could turn out.

"Aight, you got that. I'll see you on the plane." I hung up on her, and pulled into Micah's driveway. Parking my car next to my brother's, I made my way inside.

Being that we were having a meeting, I already knew where to go. Heading down the stares to the man cave, I knocked and Micah opened the door.

"Finally. You have no sense of time, dawg. I thought you were working on that," he said, closing the door behind me.

"I'm here ain't I? Lets get this shit started," I spat. Taking a seat next to Karma by the bar, I reached for the bottle of 1942 that sat in the back, and poured myself two shots. No one said anything, as I tossed them back one after the other, and slammed the shot classes on the counter.

"Aight, motherfucka, whatever you break yo' ass definitely gon' buy it back with interest." I waved him off and went to pour another shot when Karma put his hand on the glass.

"Chill out, fuck is your problem?"

"Nothing."

"Then why you throwing these shots back like a hoochie mama?" Micah bust out laughing while Karma joined in.

"I'm not in a laughing mood right now." Putting the top back on the bottle, I returned it to its place on the bar.

"We can see that. What's your problem?" Micah questioned.

"This shit with Amanda and this dumbass loyalty she got with this nigga that like the same sex as her is starting to piss me off.

"Wait, time out," Micah gestured with his hands, "Aaron like who?"

"Other niggas," Karma jumped in.

"Nahh, forreal?"

"We saw him hugged up with a nigga down at Karma's. Yet she's giving me a hard time."

"That's wild. And I've been around that man on a couple of occasions. I never got that vibe off him."

"Down low dudes never give off the vibe. It's called down low for a reason. Fuck all that though. Amanda keep hollering that she's tryna figure things out in her relationship. In my mind, they don't have one."

"Bro, on some real shit, you need to give her some time. I get that you feeling her, shit, borderline in love with the girl, but you gotta let her process shit on her end the way she see fit." I wasn't feeling the shit that Micah had to say but I understood. "When she's ready, she'll come to you."

"She gon' come running when she find out that nigga out here sneaking dicks," Karma added. "Yo, you think they still fucking?"

"I don't even wanna think about that shit. Let's get to this meeting. We all good for the meeting with Juan when we get out there?"

"Yea, we gon' head over there soon as we get the ladies settled in. I wanna get that over with and situated to be sent home before we really start our vacation," Micah advised.

I rubbed my hands together and nodded my head. I loved re up time. It was something about seeing those white keys sparkle as they were freshly packed away.

"We flying private?" I asked Micah. He lit one of his cigars and puffed on it.

"Don't we always?"

I chuckled. "Yea, boss shit only." We sat around chopping it up for another hour, before Kelly announced that Domonique and Amanda had arrived. I was the first one to start walking upstairs. I passed the kitchen where the women were talking to head to the living room.

"Hello to you too, Kaiser," I heard Domonique say.

"Yea, how you gon' walk through my house without saying hello?" Kelly co signed. "Are we not being nice today, Kaiser?"

I laughed and doubled back to the kitchen. "My bad y'all, my mind was somewhere else." Hugging both Kelly and Domonique, I gave Amanda a head nod and a quick wassup before heading back out. She wanted to be on some friend shit, I planned to act accordingly.

16

DOMONIQUE

"Ooh, bitch, not the wassup for his wife," I said once Kaiser left the kitchen. I looked over at Amanda who tried to look unbothered, but I could tell Kaiser being dry with her stung a bit.

"Right," Kelly added. "What's going on with y'all?"

"What you mean what's going on with us?" Amanda questioned; her tone a little rough.

"I'm just saying I've never seen him be so dry with you. Seems like there's some tension."

"There's no tension. Kaiser is clearly in one of his moods, and I'm not about to feed into it. If he's gonna act like that the whole trip then he better stay away from me. I have too much of my own shit going on." She rolled her eyes and I caught the hint of sadness.

"You know what, nevermind." I stopped myself before being honest with her. We were still building on our friendship and I didn't wanna say anything that would turn her off. It didn't mean that I wasn't willing to be real, it just meant that I had good timing. That's where women messed up when they were building new friendships. They felt like they could say anything that came to their mind because they were being "real". The only thing with that is that every situation doesn't call for your "real" opinion unless asked.

"What were you gonna say?" She asked.

"Nothing, I don't wanna overstep," I said respectfully.

"I promise you're not. It may be something that I need to hear." I watched her facial expression to gauge whether or not she was being sincere, and she was.

"Wait," Kelly said before I could start talking. Just as she said that, both Karma and Micah walked into the kitchen.

"Why y'all got quiet all of a sudden?" Micah asked while walking toward Kelly with a smirk on his face. He wrapped his arm around her neck from behind, and pulled her head back to kiss her.

"Judging by the look on Manda's face, they were probably in here talking about my brother," Karma said with a smirk of his own. "Wassup, beautiful." He held his arms out for a hug, and I embraced him. He kissed me on my neck, making me giggle.

"Hey, handsome."

"Ain't nobody talking about your brother. He walking around here with a stick up his ass," Amanda blurted out.

"Nah, that would be yo—" Kaiser appeared out of nowhere and Karma cut him off before he could finish his sentence.

"Bro!" Karma bellowed.

"Don't be in this bitch talking about me behind my back, Manda."

"Shut up, Kaiser. You sound so childish," she fired back.

I looked back and forth between the two as they had their little spat and couldn't help but smile. They didn't know how cute they looked. For two people who weren't a couple, they could've fooled me.

"Alright, back to your corners, fighters," Kelly said. She turned to Micah who was getting a kick out of Amanda and Kaiser as well. "Babe, it's time for us to start heading out. Seeing what's going on between these two," she pointed to Amanda and Kaiser, "I think it's best that the guys ride with you and the girls will ride with me."

"Shit, why? We already gotta be on the plane together," Kaiser jumped in.

"And I'm rethinking that," Amanda said smartly.

"Well then, go get yo ass a plane ticket and fly Jet Blue," he countered.

I couldn't hold my laughter in any longer. "I'm sorry y'all, he stupid. Karma can you help me get my luggage in Kelly's car? I'll meet y'all outside." Hopping down off the bar stool, Karma took my hand in his and we walked out. "You think they gonna be at it the whole week?" I asked Karma while we removed my bags from my trunk.

"If Amanda keeps allowing him to get under her skin, yes."

"What happened?"

"You gotta ask ya girl that, ma. What I talk about with the guys, will never go outside of us."

"I respect that." I was glad that he didn't tell me because that would've been a turn off. "Have you been to Columbia before?"

"Yea, a couple times. You?"

"Nope, it'll be my first time."

"It'll be a lot of first times on this trip," he said with a sneaky undertone while smirking. I didn't bother asking what it meant because I liked surprises.

"Were you able to load everything, Dom?" Kelly called out from the front door.

"Yep. Y'all ready?"

"Yea, we're coming out now." Each of us had two bags and a carry on. You could always count on me to overpack and be overly prepared.

"I'll see you at the airstrip," Karma said, leaning in to kiss my cheek.

"We flying private? Oh, nevermind, boss shit right?"

"Always, beautiful." I watched as he walked over to Micah's truck and hopped into the passenger seat. That boss shit turned me on, and the jumping of my clit confirmed it.

THE PLANE RIDE WAS LOVELY. I sat with Karma at his request, and slept most of the way. When we stepped off the plane that heat hit my body, and I knew for sure that we were on an island. We all piled into a black Escalade that awaited us to drive to the private house Micah had rented for the weekend. Kaiser and Amanda seemed to be on better terms and were engaging in conversation. I took that as a sign of good things to come.

"Ooh, this some fly shit," I said as we pulled up on the property. The palm trees that surrounded the villa style home were beautiful.

"Girl, I was just thinking that. How many rooms does this place have?" Kelly asked as we stepped out of the truck.

"It's three floors, seven bedrooms, and fifteen bathrooms," Micah answered. "It's a bunch of other shit in here too. We have three maids, and a butler. We're gonna do a quick tour then me and the fellas have to run out for a few. When we come back, we can have dinner. Bae, we on the first floor." He took Kelly's hand in his and escorted her away from the group.

"I bet they sneaking off to have sex," I said and Karma nodded his head in agreement.

"Shit, I'm bout to tour this shit myself and get some action," Kaiser blurted out, causing Amanda to whip her head in his direction. "Don't even start. Come on, we got the third floor." He walked ahead of her, and she stomped away following him.

"They need therapy," Karma commented. "I guess that puts us in the middle. We can take a look around and have the workers grab our bags." He held his hand out for me to grab, and we walked inside together.

The place was a realtor's dream. The beautiful archways as we walked in caught my eye, making me slow up my walk as I took in the scenery. I followed Karma up the spiral steps to the second floor, and we were greeted by one of the maids. Only she didn't look like the help to me. She looked more like a stripper and the uniform seemed to be one of her costumes.

"It's nice to see you again, Señor Karma." She batted her brown eyes and pushed a piece of her long brunette hair to the back of her ear. Her English was clear enough for me to pick up on the flirtation in her voice. She was real familiar.

"Nice to see you too, Esmeralda. This is Domonique, my guest for the week. I expect you to treat her just as well as you treat me when I'm here, if not better."

Glancing in my direction, she sized me up and gave a fake smile. "Absolutely, Señor Karma. We'll make sure that your friend gets the royal treatment." She put emphasis on the word friend. I smirked at the fact that she thought she was doing something. Unfortunately for her, I wasn't the least bit intimidated.

"I'll accept nothing less," I said with the same tone. "Can you show us to our room?"

"Oh, sure." We walked down the long hallway where she stopped at the first room that looked like a modern museum. From the massive California king size bed to the sunken in sitting space. The soft undertones that were chosen for the paint on the walls went well with the décor. "Señor Kaiser, will you be sleeping in your normal quarters for this week?"

"No, he'll be rooming with me, ain't that right, Señor Karma?" I turned to him and he walked behind me, grabbing me by my waist.

"Yea, that's right," he replied smoothly. He didn't let onto the fact that I had changed the plans I initially set on the plane, which were for us to have our own rooms.

It was too soon for me to be on this trip so it was for sure too soon to be rooming together. Seeing how this chick was basically tryna fuck him in front of me, I had to make an executive decision. Her eyes dropped in disappointment, but she perked back up real quick.

"Oh, okay. Well, I'll have Julio bring up your bags so that you can get settled in."

"Thank you, Esmeralda," I said with an added smile. Once she left the room, Karma bust out laughing.

"Yo, you're a trip," he laughed, unwrapping his hands from my waist.

"And she's a hoe. Which side of the bed are you taking?" I asked, removing my shoes and walking further inside the room, over to the bed.

"You were serious?"

"Yes. I can already tell from the interaction that y'all either fucked or you let her suck you off. I can't be mad at that because we're not even on that level. While I'm here though, the only woman you'll be entertaining is me."

He smirked while walking over to me. Standing in front of me, I could smell the Winter-fresh gum he'd popped in his mouth when we exited the plane. Him being so close made my body shiver.

"You sure you can handle sleeping in the same bed with me?"

"It depends, are you a cuddler?"

"Yea. I like to cuddle naked though."

I swallowed hard, thinking carefully about my response. He was starting to make it hard for me to behave like I'd told myself I was going to. I thought about what my therapist said about giving things a chance. Fuck it, YOLO. I stepped closer, and covered his lips with mine. I allowed him to slip his tongue in my mouth, and explore every part of it. His kiss was perfect, gentle, and when he grabbed the back of my neck, I kissed him harder. A knock on the door startled me, causing me to jump back.

"Yo, it's time to roll," Kaiser shouted from the other side of the door.

"Aight, I'll be down in a minute," Karma responded while caressing the back of my neck. I felt my nipples harden in my t-shirt and I was thankful that I'd worn this oversized shirt.

"You got two minutes. If you not downstairs by then yo ass getting left," Kaiser spat. It was clear that him and Amanda were still at it. His ass was definitely salty.

Karma went to kiss me again, and I stopped him. "Go head and handle your business. I'll be right here when you get back. Well, maybe not right here. I wanna go for a swim before dinner, so if I'm not here, you can find me there."

"Cool." He pecked my lips. "We won't be gone long."

"Okay. Do you want me to put your stuff away?"

"Nah, don't worry about that. We got people for that."

"Oh, if it's a decision between Esmeralda putting your things away and me, don't worry I'll make the decision for you."

He laughed and headed for the door. "I appreciate it. I'll see you in a few." He left out, closing the door behind him, and I fell back on the bed. We'd shared our first kiss and my fresh ass was already thinking about the positions I wanted him to put me in. This trip was certainly gonna put some things in perspective for me. I couldn't wait to see where my mind was by the end of it.

17

KARMA

I made it downstairs just as Micah and Kaiser were getting ready to leave out the door.

"Damn, its like that? Y'all niggas was just gon' leave the kid?" I jogged down the steps, and over to the front door.

"Nah, we was gonna wait for you in the car. You know I like to get to the meets at least twenty minutes before time," Micah spoke while dapping me up.

"Oh, I thought this nigga was being a hater when he came knocking on the door." I pointed to Kaiser who mugged me.

"Nigga ain't nobody hating on you. You were in there cupcaking and I had to let you know that we were on a timed schedule," he replied.

"Now tell me that wasn't some hating ass shit you just said."

"I gotta agree with him on that one, bro. You sound a little salty," Micah agreed with me.

"Mann, both of y'all shut the hell up and lets roll. Micah toss me the keys." Kasir held his hand out and Micah shook his head no.

"Nah, you not driving with that attitude. You know we gotta go through those windy roads to get to Juan's estate." Micah made that clear and walked around to the drivers side of the E Class Benz that he kept here for our short visits.

"Yea, and you ain't riding shot gun either. Get in the back and figure your shit out. You know we gotta be on point pulling up on this nigga." Now wasn't the time for him to let his shit with Amanda spill over into the business.

"First off, stop tryna lil' boy me. And second, my shit is figured out, its y'all niggas with the problem. I'ma get in the back only because I'm not driving."

"Aight," I responded, skipping over the possible argument. During the forty five minute drive to Juans estate, we were all quiet. We usually didn't talk when we were headed to take care of business. For me, I always wanted to be focused on the task at hand. We'd never had an issue when it came to our transactions with Juan, but you could never be too careful, especially when you were on someone else's turf.

We had to drive through a small town before we got to Juan's estate which, like the place we were staying for the week, was off of a dirt road. The only difference was the windy roads we had to go through to get to his place. The roads were so narrow that if you hadn't learned how to navigate them, you'd end up over the cliff.

"I'll never get used to this shit," Micah said as we pulled off the road and onto Juan's estate.

"Me either. All the money this nigga got, he need to get with the city and make the roads big enough for two cars at least." We drove past a couple guards before being stopped at the gate. Micah rolled down his window, and gave his name. After confirming our visit through a walkie talkie, we were allowed entry.

The gate opened, and we drove up the circular driveway and parked. Stepping out of the car, I could see Juan standing on the second floor balcony with his arms wide open.

"My guys, welcome back to my home," he said loud enough for us to hear.

"Thanks for having us, Juan."

"Come inside, I'll be right down." We followed behind one of two of his security detail, into the house. "Karma, my guy, how's business?" He asked as he descended the steps. This nigga Juan may have loved dressing up more than a woman. The silk button up and matching pants coordinated down to his shoes.

"Business is great. How are you, Juan?" He walked up and gave us all a brotherly hug, saving Micah for last. He always did that shit. I assumed it was a sign of respect for the boss of our operation. Micah hated it seeing as he saw me and Kaiser as bosses equally.

"I'm fantastic. Let's eat and talk business, shall we?"

"We're here for the business only. We have guests back at our place that we need to get back to," Micah announced.

"I see, no problem, Micah. We'll do business and what do you say, rain check for food?"

"Sounds good." He led us into an office where he conducted his meetings, and Kaiser did a run down of the current numbers. I hadn't seen my brother in action in a while and I had to say, he was on his shit.

"Micah, with the way you're moving this shit, you could afford to triple the amount of product you're getting now," Juan pointed out.

I agreed in my head, but I knew Micah wasn't going for it. We'd already discussed him wanting to completely get out of the game after all he'd gone through with Tracey in the past year.

"Nah, we're good where we are. I need the same order delivered on the fly. Here's where I need it to dock." Micah pulled a small piece of paper from his pocket and handed it over to Juan. Juan slid the paper into his shirt pocket and nodded his head.

"No problem. You let me know if you change your mind." He held his hand out, and Micah shook it. "Karma, Kaiser, always good to see you." We shook hands and the meeting was over.

Leaving the house, we headed back for the car. Meetings were usually this short and sweet. It seemed crazy that it required a trip this far but when you had the type of status we held, it was necessary. It was no way we were ever getting on any type of phone, no matter how complicated the stealth mode was supposed to be. Getting back in the car, we didn't speak until we were off of the property.

"That nigga gotta be losing customers, he presented the same offer the last time we were here," Kaiser said from the backseat.

"Yea, he got some shit going on. I ain't here to pick up nobody slack though. I'm working towards retirement," Micah made known.

Kaiser didn't respond, more than likely because he wasn't feeling the same way as of yet. I was sure that the day he and Amanda made things official he'd be persuaded.

"Now that we got the business out of the way, I'm ready to get to the vacation part," I said. "Oh, speaking of vacation, why didn't you mention that Esperanza was gonna be on duty knowing that Domonique would be here?" I asked Micah.

"Shit, the same reason why he didn't say anything about her sister being on duty as well," Kaiser let out. "I swear when Amelia came walking out of the guest room on the second floor, I almost lost it."

"I wasn't even thinking y'all, my bad. I'ma only take the blame for that though, nothing else. Ain't nobody tell y'all niggas to be around here fucking the help." Micah laughed and I gave him the finger.

"It's working in my favor so far because Domonique has insisted that I room with her. I just hope Esperanza not on no weird shit during the duration of our stay. I'd hate to have to fire her ass."

"Amelia already tried to proposition me in the bathroom. I had to shut that shit down quick," Kaiser said.

"Shit, with the way you were talking when we pulled up, I would've thought that you would've let her."

"Nah, I wouldn't disrespect Amanda like that. I may not be fucking with her like that right now but that's still my baby."

I shook my head, and didn't bother responding. My brother was crazy. Pulling back into the driveway of where we were staying, I exited the car first, and went to search for Domonique. I went to the back of the house first, since she mentioned wanting to get in the pool. I spotted the ladies laid out underneath one of the cabanas. Heading their way, I could hear them giggling about something, and cleared my throat to get their attention.

"Y'all over here talking about us?" I asked, walking over to where Domonique sat.

"We're over here minding our business, sir," Domonique let me know as I wrapped my arm around her neck.

"Yea, aight. You look good." I complimented the bathing suit she had on that looked like a cut up one piece. I don't know what kind of oil she had on her body but her skin was glistening.

"Thank you."

"Where are the guys?" Kelly asked.

"They should be inside. We just got back. Y'all tryna go out for dinner or have something made here?"

"How about we send the butler out to get groceries and we can make a meal here for our first night?" I liked Kelly's suggestion better than going out.

"We can send Amelia and Esperanza out for groceries. You know, seeing as they're the maids," Amanda suggested, making Domonique laugh.

"That makes so much sense girl," she cosigned.

"Whatever y'all want. Let me go let the guys know." I left

them to talk amongst themselves, and went to find Kaiser and Micah.

"Looking for me?" Esperanza asked, appearing out of nowhere.

"Nah, not at the moment, but since you're here, I need you to go out there and get a grocery list from the ladies."

"Groceries?" Her accent was heavy and she frowned up her face. "I don't shop for groceries. I do the housework, remember? I still do that other thing you like too." She licked her lips and batted her eyes.

"And I'ma show him something he gon' love. You better get the fuck on Joseline Hernandez." I don't know when Domonique walked up, but the way she stepped in made my dick rock up. Beautiful was on some gangsta shit and I liked it.

Esperanza didn't want any problems, so she sucked her teeth and went out to do what I asked. "Can we talk about that thing I'ma love?"

"Yea, at some point during this trip I'm sure we will. We're on vacation boo, anything can happen." She gave me a peck on the lips and went back outside. Domonique didn't know it but she was gon' get this work. And I wasn't just talking about physically. I wanted to get her mentally as well.

18

AMANDA

Chilling with the girls was a perfect distraction from Kaiser. The way he'd been carrying on was pissing me off, and I'd be damned if I let him ruin this vacation for me. Seeing Esperanza walking out to the backyard with Domonique behind her, I sucked my teeth. It was bad enough that me and Kaiser were at it, now I had to be in the same house as a bitch I knew he fucked. Come to find out that Amelia and Esperanza were sisters and Domonique was dealing with the same situation as me.

"Señor Kaiser said that you had a grocery list for the market," Esperanza said while stopping in front of me and Kelly.

"We do, but its not written down so I hope you have a good memory," I responded and Kelly snickered. It may have seemed like I was on some mean girl shit, but I wasn't. I gave her a run down of the ingredients I would need for shrimp linguine and she hurried off.

"I gotta watch that hoe," Domonique said as she returned to her seat. "Why I walked in the house and she was practically offering her pussy to Karma."

"Shieettt, y'all better than me," Kelly spoke. "I'll be damned if I sleep under the same roof that Micah done stuck his dick in. I'd be ready to bat the bitch upside her head."

"That's easy for you to say, Kelly, Micah is your man," Domonique countered.

"Yea, well, it's all the same to me," Kelly replied.

"Do y'all think I'm leading Kaiser on?" I asked out of the blue. Domonique stared at me while Kelly took slow sips of her drink and watched me over her glass.

"What do you think?" Domonique threw my question back at me.

"I don't know, that's why I'm asking y'all. I mean, I'm not trying to."

"I think you need to be honest with yourself about what you want," Kelly said. "Do you think that your relationship with Aaron is worth hanging in there for a little while longer?"

"No," I answered with no hesitation.

"Well damn, you didn't think about that response at all."

I chuckled a little. "It's because I've been trying to hold on to what Aaron and I used to have. At this point in my life, I no longer want to hold onto dead things, you know what I mean?"

"I know exactly what you mean, and I understand. At the end of the day you have to do what's best for you. Even if that means making changes that hurt." I nodded my head in agreement. I knew that my decision to be done with Aaron didn't come easy to me. I'd let a lot build up, so I knew that I was ready.

"Well, I know you might not wanna hear it, but I think that Kaiser is just what you need to live again."

"I believe that too, but I want to be able to accept him fully once I'm done with Aaron. I'm telling y'all this here, but I've yet to tell Aaron, and I wanna do that in person."

"I think that's a good idea," Kelly agreed. I was happy to have friends that didn't tell me what they felt I wanted to hear. I respected their honesty in that they wanted me to make decisions that were best for me in the end.

After our conversation, I felt that I needed to have a conversation with Kaiser. I might not have shown it, but I was in my feelings behind him brushing me off. I wasn't used to him being short with me, and talking to me out the side of his neck. Standing up, I put my arms into my coverup, and left it open so that my bikini was on full display.

"Where you going?" Domonique asked, taking a sip of her drink.

"She going to find her man," Kelly answered for me. She winked her eyes, and put her shades on. I snickered and kept right on stepping because that's exactly what I was going to do.

Making my way inside, the first place I went to check was his bedroom. Surprisingly, he didn't try to room with me like I thought he would've. Once we made it to the second floor, he pointed directly across from the room he deemed his, and told me that it would be my sleeping quarters for the week. His door was slightly ajar, and I could hear him barking out orders to someone on the phone. I could've taken that as a hint that he might not be in the mood to talk, but I wanted to get this off my chest. I knocked twice, and waited for him to answer.

"Get the fuck away from my door, Amelia!" He yelled out, and that made me giddy inside. It also made me want to go find Amelia's ass and beat her the fuck up. Instead, I pushed the door open, and made my presence known. "Aye, do what I said and I'll call you back later for an update," he said to whoever was on the phone before hanging up and throwing it on the bed. "If you coming in here to say some shit I don't wanna hear, save it because I'm not in the mood."

I swallowed air, and willed myself not to squeeze my legs together. There he sat on the edge of the bed, shirtless, and in a pair of basketball shorts. His dreads were wrapped up, held by a rubber band on the top of his head. My eyes scanned his entire body, stopping at his feet. This man even had nice feet. If this was a sign from God, that I needed to start listening a little harder.

"I didn't come in here to start no shit with you. I actually wanted to talk to you for a minute."

"Aight, shut the door. I'm bout to jump in the shower, so if you wanna talk, you gotta come in there." He stood up from the bed, and walked towards the bathroom that was set up in his room, similar to mine.

"Okay," I responded with no hesitance in my voice. I followed behind him, into the bathroom. When he went to step out of his shorts, I knew he expected me to turn my head, but I did the opposite. Instead, I put down the toilet seat, and sat down. He shrugged his shoulders, and dropped his boxer briefs next. "Mmm," I whispered when his dick fell out. It was a beautiful sight to behold. He had to be at least eight inches soft. It was thick, and begging to be touched, but I kept my composure.

"Stop looking at my dick witcho fresh ass," he called me out and snickered. "What you wanna talk about ma?" Turning the shower on, he stepped inside.

"I wanted to talk about where we stand. I've decided that I'm done with Aaron." I stopped talking, and waited to see what his reaction would be. When he didn't say anything, I continued talking. "I could lie and say that I don't have feelings for you, but I won't. In an ideal situation, I would work towards pursuing a relationship with you, but my situation isn't ideal. I was with Aaron for years, and I think before I jump into anything with you, I need to go through the process of purging who I was when we were together. I'm open to us being close though, and at times I will flirt with you openly, and I may be very territorial when it comes to other women. I'm just asking that you give me time."

He didn't respond for another five minutes. When he finally turned the shower off, I grabbed his towel off the back of the door to hand it to him. The shower door slid open, and my eyes went right to his now hard dick. I don't know what he was doing in there while I was talking, but his shit was rocked up.

"Pass me that towel," he said in a low voice.

"Did you hear what I just said?" I asked.

"Yea." That wasn't the response I expected, but I sucked in my emotions and handed him the towel anyway.

"Well, that was all I had to say." Opening the bathroom door, I started to head out.

"Damn, you not gonna give me a chance to respond?" He asked from behind me.

"Kaiser, stop playing, forreal." I punched him in his chest, and he pulled me in for a hug. The hug was so soothing, I didn't care that his chest was still damp.

"I appreciate you for coming in here, and being straight up with me. I respect the fact that you need to go through your process, just as long as I get to still be around. I know I joke a lot, but on some real shit, I think I love you." I went to pull myself from his embrace, but he held me tighter. "Hold on, let me get this out. I've watched you for the last couple years and I want you to know that I see you. Do what you gotta do for self. We'll be here when you're ready." He thrusted his hips towards me and I felt his dick graze my thigh.

"You so nasty." Pulling back, we locked eyes, and for the first time, I leaned in to kiss his lips. It felt so right, that I let him spread my lips with his tongue. I felt my nipples harden against the mesh material of the bathing suit. Getting deeper into the kiss, he stopped abruptly.

"Aight, you gon' have to get up outta my room before you end up bent over that dresser," he let out, while tightening the towel around his waist. I don't know if it was the kiss or him professing his love for me that made me so bold, but I put my hands on my hips, and slowly shimmied out of my bikini bottoms. He licked his lips, never taking his eyes off of me.

"What if I want that now? Quickly catching on, he dropped

his towel and swooped me up in his arms, flipping me so that I was eye level with his dick and my pussy was in his face.

I felt him blow on my pussy and braced myself for what was to come. When he latched onto my clit and began to softly suck on it while making slurping sounds I thought for sure that I was gonna pass out from the intense pleasure. Kaiser was eating my pussy like he had something to prove to me. I felt myself getting wetter by the second.

"Oooh, shit, Kaiser. Ahh fuck, eat that pussy, mmm." I couldn't concentrate with the way he was methodically rolling his tongue around every inch of my mound. I watched as his dick jumped and I took that as a sign that it was calling for my attention. Spitting on it, I let my hand glide along his shaft before taking him into my mouth, which made him further dig into my pussy.

"Mmmm," he moaned, causing a vibrating feeling to my pussy. I bobbed up and down on his dick, making sure that my mouth stayed nice and wet. The harder he went, the more I sucked, but I was no match for him. Kaiser had been waiting for this moment and it showed. Feeling myself reach my peak, I found myself trying to take all of him down my throat and popping him back out slowly.

"Ughh, I'm cumming," I announced. He didn't let up until I rained down on his face. "Ooh, ooh." My legs shook, and I held onto him for dear life, not wanting to fall.

"Damn, that pussy taste even better than I thought it would," he said, letting me down. I couldn't help but to attack his lips again, wanting to taste myself.

I was beyond turned on sucking my juices off of his lips and tongue. Hell, I was still shaking from that intense orgasm. I hadn't had enough of him and what better time to finally give in then in Columbia. Especially since I knew I wouldn't be sleeping with Aaron any longer.

"Is this how you pictured me bent over?" I asked as I walked over to the dresser and assumed the position. After all the time I wasted with Aaron, he was gonna get EVERY BIT of what he wanted.

With his manhood in his hand slowly stroking it, he slowly walked over to me and started sucking on the back of my neck. I about lost it again when he reached around and grabbed the front of my neck. His left hand lightly grabbing my throat and his right hand rubbing that beautiful thing against my ass had me wet all over again. At this point, I wanted him to feel as good as I did.

"You didn't answer me. Is this how you wanted me bent over?" I asked again in a sensual voice while I poked my butt out a little more.

"Hell yeah", he responded grabbing my neck a tad tighter. I couldn't wait any longer to feel him so I reached my right hand behind me to help him guide his way inside of my soaking wet walls. Once he slid the head in, i thrusted back on him.

"YES" I moaned and bit my bottom lip. That first stroke hit every pleasure point that it possibly could, catching me off guard in pure ecstasy. My juices began to run down my thigh after the second stroke.

"Fuck! I swear this was worth the wait" he blurted in between moans as he continued to stroke me long and slow. "I'm gonna take care of your heart and all this goodness between your legs". He kept his left hand around my neck, and was grabbing my waist with his right. I tightly held on to the dresser out of pleasure and to keep my balance while he hit it from the back while simultaneously making sure my arch was flawless. Those steady strokes had tears in my eyes. I was going to cum again if he kept going at this pace but i needed this nigga to cum for me first.

"Cum for me daddy" I cried out trying to hold in this second orgasm. At this point, his frequent moans were telling me he was close. I started to tighten my kegel muscles as hard as I could.

Four strokes later all i heard was, "Aaaahhhh! Fuck!". I immediately slid off his penis to catch his cum in my mouth. Not a minute later he was unloading all over my tongue and I could do nothing but smile. I started thinking about how dope it would be to have mind blowing sex like this regulary with someone i knew would treat me right.

"That was amazing," I gushed while walking towards the bathroom to rinse the remaining semen from my mouth and dry my face. I then rejoined him near the dresser.

"It damn sure was." He held onto the dresser getting his bearings back together and we just stood there, staring at each other until a knock on the door broke our gaze. "Dammit, who is it?"

"Y'all loud in there," I heard Domonique say, followed by a fit of chuckles. A bunch of grown ass people listening to other grown people have sex. I couldn't help but laugh myself.

"Mind y'all business," I yelled back, making them laugh harder. Kissing Kaiser again, I bent down to pick up my panties. "I'm gonna go out, you good?"

"Yea, I'm straight. I'm sleeping with you tonight?"

"Will Amelia be okay with that?" I teased.

"She ain't got no choice but to be. She lucky we ain't really fucking yet. The way I'd have you screaming would make her wanna jump off one of these balconies." He grabbed me by my ass and pulled me to him. There were those damn butterflies.

"You crazy. I'm gonna throw some clothes on. Meet me downstairs, we decided to make dinner tonight instead of going out."

"Aight." I opened the door expecting the gang to still be standing there listening, but the coast was clear for me to walk over to my room.

I hadn't checked my phone since we landed, and I was almost positive that I had a threatening message from my mother. She'd stressed that I made sure to call her soon as I got off the plane. Going through my bag, I pulled out the phone only to find it dead. Plugging it up to charge, I stripped out of the little clothing I had on, and headed for the shower. Letting the water hit my body, I found myself smiling. I had a freeing feeling after allowing Kaiser to taste me. I could see myself doing it a couple more times before the trip was over.

After spending twenty minutes in the shower, I stepped out and wrapped a fluffy towel around my body. Checking my phone again, the notifications popped up on the screen. I had two missed calls and a text from my mother, and surprisingly, a text message from Aaron. I responded to my mother first letting her know that I arrived and would be calling her soon. Opening Aaron's message, I read it twice to let his words sink in.

A: Hey, I wanted to reach out and tell you that I love you. I know things between us have been off lately and I take the blame for that. When I get back we have a lot to discuss. I'm ready to put everything on the table so that we can have a clean slate and move forward.

The message seemed encrypted and I tried my best to read between the lines. I felt a mix of emotions, but the one that didn't resonate with me was hopeful. I wasn't hopeful that he'd want to rekindle the flame that once burned in our relationship. I wanted to end it with no hard feelings. I decided not to respond, opting to handle my problems when I got back to New York. I went to set the phone down, when it rang with a call from him. I could've ignored it, but if the opportunity presented itself to face Aaron sooner than later, I might as well cease it. Tapping the screen, the call connected and I heard rattling in the background before voices became clear.

"What you not gonna do is keep using my house as a rest stop while you're getting your shit together back at home." I heard what sounded like a woman's voice on the other end of the phone, prompting my antennas to go up.

"Look, I got enough going on when I'm there, I don't need to come here listening to your bullshit too," Aaron responded.

"Well as long as you're here and choose not to leave, you're gonna hear what the fuck I gotta say," the woman responded. "You need to tell her what it is, or make this your last time coming here. I came out of the closet a long time ago. I refuse to be pushed back into one because you can't man up and accept yourself for who you are."

The words coming out of the closet echoed in my ear and I felt myself getting dizzy. Coming out? Was Aaron gay? What the hell did I just hear?

19

KAISER

After the moment that Amanda and I had shared, I didn't expect her to be all over me, but at least acknowledge a nigga. She did the exact opposite once she joined all of us in the kitchen. She went straight to the ladies, and they walked off without saying anything to us.

"Damn bro, what happened?" Karma asked.

"Hell if I know. We was just in there—." I stopped myself before going into detail about what happened behind closed doors.

"We heard what y'all was in there doing. No need to go into details." Micah chuckled and I smirked.

"Yea, well, I don't know what happened in the last few minutes. I ain't gon' sweat it though." Amanda wasn't gon' drive me crazy on her rollercoaster of emotions. I chopped it up with the guys while waiting for the ladies to return and start dinner.

"Yo, y'all think Amanda know that nigga a homo?"

"That was random as hell," Karma replied, "but nah, I don't think she knows."

"She'd probably be in jail for real. I'm still stuck from the news so imagine how she'll be when she finds out," Micah added.

"When she finds out what? And who is she?" Kelly asked, walking back into the kitchen with the girls behind her.

"Stay out of grown folks business, bae," Micah said with a straight face before bussin' out laughing. Kelly punched his arm and he pulled her to him.

"You was about to get cussed out."

"You know I'm just fucking witchu. Everything alright?" He asked. I glanced in Amanda's direction and her facial expression was one mixed with confusion and sadness.

"It will be," she responded. By the look on Amanda's face that response wasn't good enough for me.

I went to walk in her direction and seeing me come, she shook her head no as if she was telling me that this wasn't the time. I made a detour and walked out the kitchen. My phone buzzed in my pocket as I made my way out to the backyard. Reaching for it, there was a text message from Ariane. Opening the message there was a photo for me to download along with a message. I tapped the screen to download the image and read the message.

Ariane: You can quit me but you can't quit what we've created.

The image downloaded and clear as day, I could see a First Response pregnancy test on the screen. Ariane had me pegged as a clown ass nigga if she thought for a moment I believed that she was pregnant by me. As I went to text her back, I felt someone walk up behind me, making me turn around quickly. Seeing that it was Amanda, I sucked my teeth and turned back around.

"I'm not mad at you," she let out, making me snicker.

"I know you ain't mad at me. I ain't do shit to make you mad," I said without turning to face her.

"Can you turn around so I can talk to you, Kaiser?"

"I don't feel like talking right now." In my phone, I texted

Ariane, letting her know that I was gonna pull up on her once I was back in the town and that she had to take a test in front of me. Putting my phone away, I turned to walk by Amanda, only for her to block my path.

"Well, I need to talk to you, so stop acting like an ass. I—." My ringing phone cut her off before she could speak. It was Ariane calling. Shaking my head, I ignored the call and focused back on Amanda.

"Go head."

"You sure you don't need to get that?"

"Positive. Go head and get what you need to get off your chest."

"So, I just got some unexpected news. News that I'm sure wasn't meant for me to hear and I'm really just trying to process it all."

"Ooookay," I dragged out, trying to understand where she was going with her conversation. "What kind of news?" I pressed. She sat on the edge of my bed and put her hands up to her face. Now I was concerned. Walking closer, I used my hand to lift her chin. "Don't back out on me now."

"I think Aaron is cheating on me with a man," she admitted. My face screwed up but not because of the news, but more so because she considered his action cheating.

"How he cheating on you when you just said you made the decision to end it?"

"Yes, I made the decision, but I haven't officially told him yet. And is that the only thing that you heard? I said he's cheating on me with a man."

"Yea, that's fucked up." I wasn't gonna admit to what I saw back at Karma's club since the cat was already out the bag.

"Kaiser!" She yelled out my name as if I wasn't standing in front of her.

"What, why you yelling?"

"Kaiser, you literally just sucked my pussy off the bone and I just told you that my soon to be ex may be cheating on me with a man. Might I add, I don't know how long it's been going on." Now that she put it that way, shit started to click. I didn't know the last time they'd been intimate and wouldn't dare ask.

"Damn," I said as the reality set in. I had been so into wanting her that I didn't think about the possibility that the nigga could've brought her back some shit while he was out doing his thing.

"Yes. I plan to get tested for everything as soon as we get back to the states. I usually do it every six months anyway and my last check up was good."

"Nah, we got a couple more days before we head back. We gon' make sure we good before we leave. Matta fact, let me make a couple calls to get us situated." Soon as I mentioned the word calls, my phone rang in my hand. Again, Ariane's name popped up, making it clear that she wasn't gonna stop calling until I said something to her.

"Can I answer your phone?" Amanda asked with a straight face. My first thought was to say no, but I wanted to see how she would handle the situation, so I handed it to her. "You sure?" She confirmed.

"Do ya thang," I responded confidently with a nod of my head. She slid the call symbol across the screen and put the phone on speaker once it connected.

Ariane's voice came through before Amanda could get a word out. "You got me fucked up if you think I'm bout to piss on another stick just to appease you. Face it, Kaiser, ya fucked with me and now your stuck with me."

I went to respond and Amanda put her finger up to her own mouth, shushing me.

"Hey, Ariane is it?" She questioned.

"Who the hell is this?"

"Kaiser's future. I'm gonna kindly ask that you no longer contact him while we're away on vacation. He promised me no distractions and I want to ensure that he keeps that promise. I'll be sure to send him your way to get your affairs squared away once we're back on U.S. soil." She casually ended the call and handed the phone back to me while standing to her feet. "I hope you didn't get that girl pregnant."

"Nah, Ariane want my attention, that's all. The only person I'm tryna bless with my seeds is you."

"You still wanna be with me after I slept with someone who slept with a fucking man?"

"Did you know he was sleeping with men?"

"Of course not."

"Aight then, I still wanna be with you." I leaned in to kiss her cheek and grabbed her hand. "Let's be clear though, anything you had with that nigga is dead once we touch down." I wasn't compromising on that now that she knew the truth.

"Without question." Nodding my head, we went back to join the crew and hopefully the rest of our vacation so long as our results came back good.

"Y'ALL REALLY OUT HERE CHEATING ME outta my money," Micah complained as we finished up a game of spades. It was him and Kelly against me and Amanda. We were killing their ass and by the look on both of their faces, neither one was too happy about it.

"Bae, that's you," Kelly pointed out. "You cut about three of my books that could've walked. I was giving you a signal with my eyes and everything." We all laughed as she did an example of her signal.

"Yo, that was the signal?" He fussed. "I damn sure missed that."

"Damn, the signal was kinda weak though, Kelz." I put my

two cents in, making her pick up one of the decorative pillows from the couch and threw it at me.

"Food is done," Domonique announced. We all made our way into the kitchen to eat. It was crazy how the women ended up on one side of the table and the men on the other. Each couple across from each other as if the seating was planned.

"Thanks for cooking tonight," I said to Domonique who spent most of her time in the kitchen. "Wait, Karma was in there with you, right?"

"Yea," she answered.

"Y'all wasn't in there doing no freaky shit, right?" She cracked up laughing while Karma shook his head. "Bro, stop playing with me. A nigga hungry as fuck right now."

"Eat your food, man," Karma said with a smirk.

I watched as everyone else put their forks to their mouths first before following suit. During the meal we sat around and talked about all that we had going on. It felt good to be around like minded people who were all about their bread. I could hear the passion in Amanda's voice as she talked about her new salon. With a drive like hers, I knew without a doubt that she was gonna be successful.

"You did your thang on this food, girl," Amanda complimented Domonique after wiping her plate clean.

"Thank you, boo. I'm glad y'all enjoyed it because it won't be happening again. We're on vacation, so I wanna be wined and dined the entire week." She looked over at Karma and winked her eye.

I tapped Amanda with my foot under the table and motioned like I was humping the air while pointing over at Amanda and Karma. She covered her mouth and chuckled. Once everyone was done eating, the men volunteered to do the dishes.

"Yo, Micah, I need you to reach out to Juan and see if he can put me in touch with an in-house doctor," I said while pouring dishwashing liquid onto a sponge.

"What you need a doctor for?" He questioned. I didn't wanna put Amanda out there, but I knew he wouldn't make the call with the kind of urgency I needed if I didn't tell him what was going on.

"Amanda got a call from Aaron a little bit ago, only he didn't know he was calling her. She knows that he's fond of both sides of the coin. We got into some shit earlier and she wants to get checked out to make sure homeboy ain't drop no shit on her."

"Shit, or you," Karma added.

"Right. Can you get that done for me asap, bro?"

"I got you," Micah assured me. "You don't seem too concerned."

"You sound like her. I can't blame shorty for shit she didn't know what's going on with dude and I think we're both good. I'm not gon' trip until I feel that there's a reason to."

"I guess that makes sense," Karma said, unsure. His phone rang and he stepped out of the kitchen to answer it.

"What you think?" I asked Micah.

"I think you're handling it better than I expected. I just hope that he didn't drop anything off. That shit would be crazy."

"We wouldn't even have time to digest it because I'd have that nigga touched whereva he at while we sitting here enjoying vacation."

"Yo," Karma called out, returning to the kitchen, "we gotta get back to the states. Somebody set Karma's on fire."

"Get the fuck outta here!"

"Making the call now. Let the girls know," Micah said, springing into action like he always did. Whoever was bold enough to set fire to my brother's establishment was gonna see why the name Karma fit him so well.

20

DOMINIQUE

W e hadn't even made it twenty four hours in Columbia before we were on a plane back to the states. I couldn't lie and say that I didn't feel a way that my vacation was cut short before it even started but I was concerned about how Karma was feeling. I knew how much work he'd put into making his club perfect. Not to mention the money he put in as well. I sat next to him in silence on the flight back home, allowing him to fully process his thoughts. I placed my hand on top of his and gave it a squeeze, letting him know that I was here.

"I'm sorry for ruining your vacation, beautiful. Soon as I get all this shit sorted out, I'ma make it up to you. And you can hold me to that," he let me know.

"Don't worry about that. I'll admit, I was a little salty but figuring out who's out to get you is way more important." He stared at me before chuckling a little. "What, why you laughing?"

"Nah, it's just funny when you say, out to get me, as if the boogeyman is coming."

"Oh," I responded oddly. "Has your manager been able to

check the video cameras? And did she notice anything going on the previous night that could have alluded to things to come? I mean, whoever started the fire must've known that you were out of town."

"I told her to hold off on checking the cameras until I got there. I could look at the feed through my phone, but I wanna get to the building to see just how much damage was done. I've been there for a minute now and haven't had any problems and I've racked up my fair share of enemies along the way. This shit do seem personal though."

I nodded my head in agreeance. Arson is usually personal, at least from my standpoint. Karma's was in a high traffic area, so whoever the culprit was had their pick of what establishments to target. So his just so happened to be the one? Nah, I highly doubt that. I only hoped that the cameras did reveal the person and they got dealt with accordingly.

Pulling my phone out of my purse, I turned it on for the first time since leaving NY. I really planned on taking this vacation seriously. I had sent out an email to all of my potential and current clients, letting them know I'd be gone for the week and would answer any and all questions or concerns once I returned. Seeing that I was returning, I planned to jump right back into work. Once the phone was powered up, I watched the email notifications and voicemails flood in. But I expected nothing less.

Clicking on the voicemail icon on my phone, I saw a message from an unknown number. Interested in knowing who the unknown caller was, I selected that message first.

"My dearest, goddaughter, how are you? I know I'm the last person you expected to hear from after all these years, but it's been long overdue. I don't wanna talk too much on your voice-mail so give me a call at 917-222-2342 as soon as you return."

When the message ended, I played it back again to make sure I wasn't losing it. I hadn't heard from this woman since she put me out for refusing to continue helping her set nigga's up. I don't even know how she got my number. The wheels in my head were spinning because Viv was known for having shit going on with her and being in the mix. What she wanted with me, I had no clue but I was gonna reach out to her when I got settled in. I wanted to meet up just so I could shit on her with my lifestyle. She needed to know that I made it without her just like I told her I would.

Getting up from my seat, I went to check on Amanda. She had found out some fucked up news not even hours before Karma got hit with his. Imagine finding out that the man that you've given years of your life to has been sneaking dick for God knows how long. I could feel the devastation in her voice and see it in her face. When she dropped that news on me and Kelly, I ain't know what to say. Walking back to where she sat next to Kaiser, I shook my head at the sight before me.

Kaiser was knocked out on Amanda's shoulder, with his mouth half way opened. She looked up at me and smiled.

"You good?" She asked.

"Yea. I was coming to check on you. I see your baby is resting though, so we'll talk when we land." I chuckled and she put her hand up to stop me from walking away.

"No, we can talk now." She nudged Kaiser a little, making him stir before opening his eyes.

"What happened?" He asked, sitting up straight.

"I need to talk to Domonique real quick."

"Oh, aight." He kissed Amanda's cheek and leaned his head against the window. The fact that he didn't mind showing affection in spite of what was going on gave him brownie points in my book. Amanda stood and we sat a row behind and across from Kaiser.

"So, how you feeling?"

"About going home early?" She asked.

"Well about that and what you're gonna have to face when you get there."

"To be honest with you, I'm ready to confront him. And as crazy as it may sound, I wanna hear what he has to say. I mean, he owes me that much."

I nodded my head in agreement. He owed her that and much more. "That's a fact. Have you talked about it with loverboy over there?" I pointed over at Kaiser who now had the cover over his head.

She chuckled before answering. "We touched on it briefly. If it was up to him, I wouldn't even go back to my place. I let him know that I needed to approach this situation head on because I'd put too much into this relationship. I did stress the importance of the both of us getting tested for STD's though. I don't wanna play with my life or his."

"Right. You a real one for that. Any other chick would've kept that information to themselves. Just know that if you need me, I'm here and I'm down for whatever. That includes and is not limited to jumping Aaron's ass if necessary." She laughed and we slapped fives.

"Thanks, boo. It sucks that we had to end our vacation so soon. Shit, it sucks even more that I got this news about Aaron. I had just gotten comfortable with the idea of letting Kaiser eat me up for the duration of our trip."

I put my hands up to cover my ears and rolled my eyes. "You could've kept that to yourself."

She smirked and pulled my hands down. "I could've but you were at the door listening, so I figured you wouldn't mind." She stuck her tongue out at me and I laughed.

"That was not my idea."

"Yea, whatever."

"Being that this vacation was a bust, we definitely have to link up for a spa day or something."

"Sounds good to me." We talked for a few more minutes before returning back to our seats once the flight attendant announced that the plane was set to land in thirty minutes.

As I walked back to my seat, Karma came towards me. "Hey, we're about to land," I said to him.

"I know. I'm headed to the bathroom real quick. For some reason, I have better cell reception in there and I need to make a call." I nodded my head, allowing him to walk past me. I took a couple steps forward before turning and following behind him.

"We see you, hot ass," Kelly whispered loudly, smacking my butt as I passed. I snickered and kept moving. I raised my hand to knock on the door and it opened before I could.

I looked up at Karma and he smiled. Gesturing with his head for me to come inside, I smiled back and entered. No words were spoken between us as he grabbed my waist and pulled me to him. He smashed his lips into mine. A tingling sensation went through my body as he manhandled me. Grabbing a handful of my ass, he squeezed and deepened the kiss.

"Mmm," I moaned into his mouth, accepting his tongue that he was practically giving away. Feeling his hand reach into the front of my pants, I stopped him. Remembering the reason I came to him, I pulled my lips from his and reached down to unbuckle his jeans. I knew he was stressing and I wanted to help him relieve some of it. Squatting down in front of him, I bared my weight down on my knees and pulled his pants down, letting them fall to his ankles. His dick sprang free from his boxer briefs and stood at attention.

Making sure my mouth was moist, I opened wide to take in all of his thickness. I allowed him to slide in and out of my mouth at a slow pace. I made sure to stare into his eyes, wanting him to see how eager I was to please him.

"Ssss, suck that motherfucka, Dom." He placed his hand on the back of my head and gently guided himself in and out of my mouth. I twirled my tongue around his mushroom head and felt my spit spilling out of the corners of my mouth. Feeling his dick tickle the back of my throat, I gagged but kept on sucking. Niggas get a kick out of that gagging shit.

"Goddamn, Dom, I'ma bout to bust beautiful." Hearing him call me beautiful while I had a mouth full of his dick made me giggle inside. Karma was a romantic gangsta. Wanting to help him reach his peak faster, I used my hand to jerk him off while sucking faster. Soon as I did, he was pulling me off of my knees and throwing his tongue back in my mouth. I could feel his hard penis rubbing against my belly. He then proceeded to reach back into the front of my pants. There was no way i was going to say no.

"I never said i wanted to join the mile-high club" I jokingly whispered in his ear as he started gently rubbing his thumb against my clit. I was trying to hold back my moans to avoid everyone hearing me on the other side of the door but I was struggling. After another two minutes, I fully gave in, unlocking my lips from his and looking down as I slipped my pants and panties off for easy access. I fully decided that I was, in fact, going to join the mile high club today. At this point, the pilot was informing us that we had 15 more minutes until landing.

"I think I can make your day better in 15 minutes", i said slyly taking on a challenge as I lifted one leg onto the sink exposing a fat yoni. Still standing there erect he responds, "I'm pretty sure you can, beautiful". He immediately proceeded to glide his already moist penis inside me. "Ohh, shit" I whispered to myself. I don't know if I was prepared for him to feel that good. His strokes were steady and strong. Feeling his breath on me with every stroke added to the already intense situation. After what felt like 2 minutes, I could feel myself losing the challenge I embarked on. I wanted to do something special for him but I was no longer in control. I was succumbing to the pleasure.

"Ohh, shit," I blurted out. Placing my hand on the sink next to my foot for sturdiness , he pumped in and out of me until I finally released. "Ahhh, ughh," I groaned and twitched. His steady pumps turned slow and deep as I finished cumming all over that hard penis. After a minute or so passed, I knew it was time to finally finish him off. With the pilot reminding us of the 10 minutes we had left to be seated, I hurried back into my last position next to my clothes on the floor. I took him back into mouth and started stroking him while I sucked.

"Damn beautiful", he moaned, throwing his head back in enjoyment. "I told you that I wanted to brighten your day a little bae", I said while steadily sucking and stroking. His penis was rock hard and his veins were poking out something serious. Knowing we were pressed for time, I sucked a little quicker with my hand still following my mouth down his shaft. I kept it going until I could tell he was reaching his peak. He looked back down at me and gently glided my head with his hand pressing into my mouth a little harder until he exploded.Swallowing, I stood and leaned over the sink to wash my mouth. He stared at me through the mirror and I smirked. My mission had been accomplished. As I went to redress and leave the bathroom, he grabbed me by the loop in my jeans.

"You tryna fuck my head up or something?" He asked with a serious face.

I giggled and shook my head. "Nah, I'm tryna get ya mind right." I winked at him before finally making my exit.

As we stepped off the plane, a chill went through my bones. It wasn't a weather related chill because it was a nice spring day. I felt like something was about to go down. Three cars awaited us at the airstrip and I gave the ladies hugs and did the same with Kaiser and Micah. Karma escorted me to a black Escalade and helped me inside where a driver awaited us. I watched out of the window as Micah and Kaiser did the same with the ladies before huddling up with Karma.

"How you doing today?" The driver spoke, looking back at

me through the rearview mirror. He was smiling hard, showing the gaps in his mouth.

"I'm fine," I answered dryly, letting him know that I wasn't in the mood to talk.

"You sho is fine," he responded back, licking his lips. I frowned up my face just as the door opened and Karma entered the car.

"What's wrong, you aight?" He asked, noticing the sour look on my face.

"Yea, I'm good." I didn't want him to get worked up and whip the driver's ass for trying to mack.

"You sure?" He asked again, skeptical of my answer.

"I'm positive." I leaned over and kissed his lips softly. The driver got the hint and began driving off.

"Where to boss?" He asked. Karma rattled off my address and the driver nodded his head.

"I'm gonna get you home and check in with you later. I hate to leave you so soon but I gotta get started figuring out what happened at the lounge."

"Karma, I get it. You don't have to explain. Take care of your business and I'll be available when you call. I hope you find out who did that wack ass shit. Let me know if you need me for anything."

"I appreciate that beautiful. All I need you to do is pick up the phone when I call. A nigga gon' need some warm legs to lay in between after the next couple days I'ma have."

"I got you boo," I assured him. The wall that I'd taken years to build was slowly crumbling after spending a little time with Karma. He was genuine and I felt at ease when I was around him. We held hands the entire drive and it didn't feel awkward. I actually initiated the hand holding. I couldn't wait to follow up with my therapist because this was progress. Pulling up to my condo, Karma let the driver know that he'd be back down in a few so that he could help me with my luggage.

"Welcome back, Ms.Domonique," my doorman greeted me as we entered my building. He insisted on being formal with me even though I had to practically force him into calling me by my first name by not responding when he called me by my last name.

"Hey, Preston. How you doing?" I spoke back.

"I'm good. A woman came by yesterday and left this for you." He handed me a small envelope. Looking at the envelope with my name spelled in cursive, I wondered who the woman may have been.

"Can you describe her to me?" He gave a brief description of the person that I instantly knew as my godmother. Thanking him, Karma and I proceeded to step into the elevator. Finding out that Viv knew where I lived didn't sit right with me. I was a grown ass woman now, so all that popping up unannounced shit wasn't gonna fly with me. The plan was to find her before she came to find me again.

KARMA

CHAPTER TWENTY ONE

After making sure Domonique got in the house safe and promising to link up later, I shook that lover boy shit off and got into gutter mode. Motherfuckas had me confused for a bitch made nigga and it was about to get real ugly out here. Fucking with my livelihood would not go over well.

"Take me to Karma's," I said to my driver. "And don't think I didn't peep you checking out my lady."

"I ain't mean no disrespect, boss."

"I'm sure you didn't, but here I'm addressing the situation with you. Any woman you see me with going forward just assume that she's mine and be mindful of those lustful looks. Looking at that one almost got your face put through the windshield." Tyler had been my driver for a while now; he knew better.

"Sorry about that."

"Don't be sorry, be careful." We locked eyes through the rearview mirror and he looked away first. I didn't want anyone that I employed to be scared of me but I wanted them to be cautious. Unlocking my phone, I went to dial Raven's number when an incoming call came in from Kaiser.

"What's the word?"

"Bro, whoever did this shit must've been scoping out the place to know when no one would be around."

"How you know that?" I questioned.

"I took the liberty of logging into your camera feed from my phone and I just watched the whole thing. A black Lincoln Navigator pulled up exactly ten minutes after Raven pulled out." My mind went to Trina. It wasn't a coincidence that not long after I had fired her some shit happened at my place of business.

"Good looking out, bro. I'm headed that way now to see what the damage looking like." My phone beeped, indicating I had a new call. Pulling the phone from my ear, I saw that it was Raven trying to get through.

"Yo, this Raven. Let me hit you back."

"Aight, keep me posted on how you plan to move. You know we gotta get this right."

"I'm already on it bro. Matta fact, meet me at my crib in two hours." I clicked over to the other line to answer Raven. "Hello."

"Where you at man? I'ma bout to act a fool out this bitch," she gritted.

"I'm on my way to you. What's going on?"

"I'm out here tryna get inside the building and they got Fire Marshall Bill here playing security. Talking about he need to speak to the owner."

"Aight, keep calm and don't interact with nobody else out there." I figured that if they had a fire investigator out there the cops weren't too far behind. "I'm twenty minutes out."

"Copy." I hung up the phone and shook my head. If it did turn out that Trina had played a part in this, she was gonna regret the day we ever crossed paths. We drove another twenty minutes before arriving at the lounge. Outside there was yellow tape around the building and my blood boiled at the sight before me. I had put big money into this lounge and to see the charred building I wanted to explode.

"Damn," I heard Tyler say, taking the words right out of my mouth. There were four cars out front, including Raven's. I watched as ATF agents walked out from the side of the building with Raven following behind them with a scowl on her face. Tyler parked the car and I hopped out.

"Keep your eyes open," I told him as I got out. I didn't trust anyone, especially any type of law enforcement.

"Sir, this is a restricted area."

"And this is my place of business," I let him know. "Let me speak to the person in charge." I could tell by the guy's demeanor that he wasn't the boss.

"Yo, do you see this shit? I can't believe this is the same building man," Raven said distraught. I appreciated the fact that she cared about my business as if it was her own.

"We gon' get this shit straightened out. Where's the person in charge?"

"The head investigator is by the employee entrance along with a detective. I don't know what these dudes were doing inside being that they were giving me a hard time." I headed that way with her following behind me.

"Excuse me, are y'all comparing notes or tryna figure out what y'all gonna eat for lunch?" I questioned the pair that stood in front of a black town car shooting the shit. They both turned towards me with dirty looks.

"And who the hell are you?" The detective in the overly starched polyester suit spoke.

"I'm the owner and also a taxpayer. Right now I'm feeling like y'all wasting my tax paying dollars standing around."

"Can I see some I.D?

"My I.D doesn't show proof that I'm the owner of this establishment."

"Sir, we don't want any trouble, we just need to see some I.D," the ATF agent stepped in. I watched as the detective put his hand on his hip, exposing his weapon. Before I could say anything about it, Raven stepped in.

"I got you," she said with her phone out to record the interaction. "He's the owner and if y'all could allow him to go inside like I asked to do, then he can show you the proof. We shouldn't have to go through all of this shit especially since this man is still digesting this." She waved her hand towards the lounge. While she spoke, I kept my eye on the detective. I wasn't about to become another notch on the NYPD's belt. Taking a deep breath, I went another route.

"Look, if I can get inside then I can show you all the proof you need. If it's still viable. Or if you feel better escorting me in, let's do that." The detective nodded his head and gestured for me to start walking. I wasn't about to let this nigga walk behind me, so I stepped to the side so that he could walk beside me instead.

Pushing the charred door open, I entered what used to be my fly ass establishment. Shit was all bad. I mentally tried to calculate the amount of damage before me, but as we walked further inside, I stopped.

"What we're looking at is a clear case of arson, Mr.—"

"Karma," I said to the ATF agent.

"Karma. The upside is although this looks bad, I've seen worse. This is more water damage than anything from what I can see. Your sprinkler system went off at the right time." He pointed to the ceiling to show me what he was talking about. I'm sure as a big time nightclub owner you'll be back up and running in no time. Do you have insurance?"

I shook my head at the last part of his statement. "We are fully insured and everything will be taken care of," I assured him. We stepped over a bunch of debris to get to my office in the back and surprisingly, the door that led to that area had held up. I typed in the code to get to the back and did the same to get into my office. Quickly grabbing my building permits to show proof of my ownership, I handed them over. "Here's the proof that you're looking for."

The ATF agent whose name I still didn't know took the paperwork and skimmed it over before handing the papers over to the detective. He gave the papers a once over before handing them back over to me.

"Do you have any enemies sir?" The detective asked.

"Can I have your names?" They willingly gave me their names. "No, I don't have any enemies."

"Who was the last person to leave the establishment?"

"My general manager, here." I pointed towards Raven. "I'm sure she let you know that already."

"I damn sure did," she added.

"She did, but we needed to hear it from you." This fucker wanted an issue with me and I could already tell by our interaction that we weren't gonna get anywhere so doing what I felt was best, I dismissed them.

"Clearly we're not getting anywhere and I can't afford to waste anymore time standing around with y'all. If you have any further questions you can reach out to my lawyer." Pulling out my wallet, I took out my lawyer's card and handed it over. "Raven, can you escort these two gentlemen out, I have some calls to make."

BEFORE THE SUN rose on the next day, I had the names of the two guys who had played a part in setting fire to my lounge. Micah had put the word out that it was fifty thousand on every nigga involved head and Kaiser got the call the same night. I asked Kaiser to send one of our people to pick the two niggas up but of course he did the exact opposite. He called me on FaceTime and there the guys lay shook, in the trunk of a Honda Accord.

"We at the warehouse," I said to him.

"Cool," he responded before slamming the trunk shut.

"Man, I told you to send someone to do that."

"I know, but nobody was available," he said while smiling as he hopped in the driver's seat of the car. I knew he was bull-shitting.

"Whatever, Kaiser. I'll see you in a minute." I hung up the phone and looked over at Micah who was shaking his head and smiling.

"Your brother is a fucking fool."

"And hard headed as shit. Aye, I meant to apologize for fucking up the trip with my shit I got going on."

"You know you don't have to apologize to me, bro. We can go on vacation at any time. We got our business done and the ladies understood so that's all that matters. Lets focus on what's going on here right now. What the insurance say about the building?"

"They'll be cutting a check for me first thing tomorrow morning so I can get to rebuilding."

"Sounds good to me. I already reached out to Tony and his team and they're ready to get started whenever you're ready."

"I appreciate that, my guy. I plan on finding out who was behind this before I start the process all over." The door to the warehouse buzzed and Micah went over to check the camera. He gave me a head nod and I pressed a button to let up the doors for Kaiser to drive through. Once he put the car in park, I made my way over to the trunk. "Pop it," I signaled to him. When the trunk popped open, the first guy's hands went up to his face.

Lifting him up by his collar, I stared dead in his eyes. He looked no older than eighteen but his eyes never wavered from mine. Rather than being scared, it seemed like he was mad about having to be here.

"Man, what's going on?" The other guy questioned, still curled up in the trunk.

"Y'all know anything about a fire down at Karma's Lounge?"

"Never heard of a Karma's Lounge," the tough guy spoke. Not in the mood to play the guessing game, I let go of his collar and put my hand around his throat and gave it a squeeze.

"Get that nigga out of the trunk, bro," I said to Kaiser. Tough guy's eyes got big and he went to pull away from me only making my grip tighter. "Honesty is always the best policy when it comes to me. Let me try another approach. Someone set fire to my lounge and all roads have led to the two of you. Now I know for a fact that you don't know the shit storm you stepped in or else you would've thought long and hard before you made that mistake. Give me the name of who put you up to it."

I loosened my grip enough for him to take in air. He glanced over at his partner and then back to me.

"I don't know what you talking bout," he spat in defiance. *CRACK!* My fist came crashing down on his jaw causing him to yell out in pain and fall to the ground. "Ahhh!"

"It was our boss, man! Come on, let my brother up," the other guy yelled out.

"Who the fuck you work for?" I asked, wanting to know who was dumb enough to hire some young ass niggas to fuck my place up.

"We not in the streets. We work at *Viv's Place*."

"Get the fuck outta here!" Kaiser exclaimed, sounding just as shocked as I was.

"You work at *Viv's Place*?" I asked for verification.

"Yea. I'm a waiter and my brother is a dishwasher."

"Okay, y'all losing me. What the hell does *Viv's Place* and Karma's being burned down have to do with each other?" Micah asked, scratching his head.

"Our mother is the owner of that bakery and i'm guessing their fucking boss." I pointed to the kid in front of Kaiser and the one of the floor, still holding his jaw. The shocked look on

Micah's face said everything without him having to verbally express himself.

"Y'all go take care of that and I'll straighten this out right here," Micah suggested, reading my mind.

"Wait, take care of what? Man, we didn't know, we thought we was helping Ms Vivian out on some insurance scam shit," the kid that was still standing pleaded. "Me and my brother have been sleeping in our car for the last month and Ms. Vivian noticed. She asked us if we wanted to make some extra money and help her out, she also promised us a place to stay. Of course we jumped at the opportunity. We were only thinking about sleeping in a bed when we accepted the offer."

"That shit supposed to make us feel better, lil nigga!" Kaiser barked, making him jump. "It's shelters out here and y'all made a decision and now you gotta live with it." He pulled his gun from his waistband and pointed it at the kid's head.

"Nooo," his brother yelled out, jumping up from the floor to protect him.

"Put the gun away, bro," I said to Kaiser in a calm tone.

"Here you go with this boy scout shit," Kaiser huffed. "So you wanna just let them go after they cost you all this money in damages and fucked up our vacation? We ain't gon give these lil' niggas no leg shot or nothing?" The disappointment in his tone would've been comical had we not been dealing with kids.

"We not shooting no kids, bro," I responded.

"These ain't no fucking kids though. These is bad ass moth-erfuckas that set your shit on fire."

"I got an idea," Micah stepped in. "Y'all lil' niggas good with y'all hands?" He asked. They both nodded their heads yes. "Aight, well consider yourselves hired. Y'all gon help with the clean up of my boy's business and we'll pay you in room and board. Micah was always thinking on his feet and his plan sounded like a good one. The reward was greater than what the outcome could've been.

"Nah, we good," the kid with the leaky nose spoke.

"You must be the youngest because that was some young, stupid ass shit to say," Kaiser spat. "Let me shoot this one."

Micah chuckled and I shook my head before responding. "What's your name, man?"

"Jackass." Kaiser's outburst made me grill him. He shrugged his shoulders.

"My name is JJ and this is my brother, PJ." He pointed to the more sensible of the two of them.

"Well JJ, I'm not sure what part of what my partner just said sounded like a request. You have no choice but to complete the tasks that will be assigned to the both of you. Either that or you can see what that leg shot feels like. It's up to you."

"We'll do the job," PJ spoke for the both of them.

"Sounds good. As of today, you no longer work at *Viv's Place*. I don't even want you going back there. My partner Micah will be setting you up from here. Let's bust a move Kaiser." Tucking his gun, he shook his head and pushed through the boys to get to the driver's side of his car. "Oh, and welcome to Karma Enterprises. You had your first infraction, there's no second chances." I made my position clear before getting into the passenger side of Kaiser's car.

"You sure about this decision you making to put them on the team?" Kaiser asked as we drove out of the warehouse. I watched the boys through the rearview mirror as they talked to Micah and nodded my head.

"Yea, I'm sure. Them lil' niggas are hungry and with proper feeding and guidance I can have some goons on my hands."

"So you just saying forget that they torched your shit?"

"Nah, I'm not saying forget it. This will be a hard lesson that they're gonna learn." Kaiser didn't get it now but he'd see.

"I still think the leg shot would've put they little asses in the right frame of mind. Or even chopping off a pinky or something. I trust that you know what you're doing though."

"Gee, thanks," I responded, sarcastically.

"Where we headed?"

"To tap in with our egg donor. She got some shit to explain. I'm not willing to be so lenient with her." Checking the clock as he drove, I noticed that it was going on ten in the morning. I expected the bakery to have high traffic but when we pulled up, there was only three cars in the driveway.

One of the cars that I noticed right away was Domonique's all white Range Rover. An eerie feeling went through my body.

"Yo, ain't that your girl's car?" Kaiser asked, parking across from it.

"Yea."

"Hmph, odd as hell. It don't seem like the place is even open today but if these cars are here someone is inside."

"I don't know but we about to find out." We both got out of the car and walked up to the building. Kaiser went to open the door and surprisingly it was unlocked.

Upon entering the place, we heard what sounded like arguing, followed by tussling coming from somewhere in the back. As we moved in that direction, the deafening sound of a gunshot stopped us in our tracks. Pop! We waited to see if any other shots would ring out before rushing further in.

"Fuck!" I heard as a door swung open and we were met by Domonique with a long scratch on her eye and a gun in her hand. We locked eyes for a moment before her head fell. What the fuck had we just walked into.

22

KAISER

Seeing Domonique standing in front of us with a gun in her hand threw me. I didn't know whether to put my hands up or applaud the fact that she was holding it like she knew what she was doing. We all stood looking at each other until I broke the silence.

"You aight?" I asked Domonique. She looked at me and her eyes glossed over. I knew then that she was in shock.

"Gimmie the gun, ma," Karma said while reaching for it. She didn't lift her hand but allowed him to take the gun from her. Tucking it away, he moved her to the side, giving me access to the room she came out of. Pushing the door open, I stepped inside and ran into my mother laid out on the floor, bleeding from her chest. Her eyes were wide open, staring at me.

I knew I was supposed to feel something but my heart felt detached from my body. I don't mean in a sentimental way either. I didn't feel anything. To be honest, I didn't know how to feel. I kneeled down to close her eyes out of respect and before I could touch her, Karma's voice stopped me.

"Bro, you can't touch her," he said. "Damn, this is fucked up. Let me call Micah." I stood up straight and shook my head.

"Check for any cameras," Domonique suggested, returning back to the room. Pulling off my shirt, I used it as a glove to prevent leaving behind any fingerprints as I checked for the cameras. Opening up a cabinet, I found high tech equipment that was easy to access. Ejecting the cd that was inside, I broke it in half and tucked it away in my back pocket.

"We gotta get outta here," Domonique voiced, sounding nervous.

"I'm witchu on that," I agreed. "This whole scene done caught a nigga off guard." Stepping around the body, we went to walk out of the room when I heard the front door open and close.

"Hey, I gotta go. You know my boss be trippin' about me being late. I'll call you on my break." It sounded like whoever had came in was on their way to the back. "Ms.Vivian, I am so sorry for being late. I know I was supposed to op...." Her words got caught in her throat due to my Glock nine pointed in her face. "Please don't kill me. I don't know where she keeps the money," she pleaded.

"No one's gonna kill you, shorty," Karma said, pulling Domonique behind him and speaking for himself. He wasn't the nigga with the gun in his hand. "When we leave, you're gonna wait five minutes and call the police."

"The police!" Domonique shrieked. I even looked at him like he'd lost his damn mind.

"You're gonna make the call and tell them that you came in late and found your boss in her office, dead. Her hand shot up to her mouth and her eyes got big.

"She's dead? Oh, hell, I don't want anything to do with this. I'll just leave and act like this never happened."

"You're here already," I cut in. "You can either do what he said or lay next to her, your choice." I don't know what was up with people playing jeopardy with their lives when making a decision to live today.

"Let me get your i.d," Karma requested. She hesitantly took her bag off of her shoulder and took out her wallet. She sucked her teeth before handing it over. Taking out the i.d he handed the wallet back over to her. "I'll be in touch in the next 48 hours. Stick to the script and I got something for you."

"And if you don't stick to the script, I got something for you." I tapped the gun against my head making sure she got my drift. She nodded her head and I put the gun away. "Cool, we out."

Walking around her, we made our way outside and to our cars. Thinking quick, I turned back around and with my shirt still in my hand, I hit the glass door making it shatter. It needed to look like someone had broken in. Jogging back over to the car, Karma let me know that he was riding back with Domonique. I was fine with that because I wanted to know what happened. What relation did Domonique have with my mother that brought us here? Getting into the driver's seat, Domonique called out to me.

"Kaiser, I'm sorry about what happened. It really was self defense." I could tell by her demeanor that she was being honest.

"You did what you had to do." Starting the car up, I drove off in the direction of Amanda's crib. I hadn't seen or heard from her since the day I dropped her off home. I tried not to read too much into it and give her space but the silence was killing me. I had to see my baby.

PULLING up to Amanda's apartment complex, I dialed her number to see if she would answer. Unlike the other few times I had called, the phone rang four times before going to voicemail. That only meant she wasn't declining the calls this time. Parking my car, I reached into the backseat and pulled out a new Lacoste shirt from the Macy's bag I had sitting on the floor. Ripping off the tag, I threw it over my head and proceeded to walk towards her building.

Taking the elevator upstairs, when the doors opened on her floor, my heart started to beat fast in my chest. The feeling made me pause for a second to gather my thoughts. Taking a deep breath, I stepped off and kept moving towards her apartment. Reaching her door, I rang the doorbell.

"Who is it?" She answered.

"It's, Kaiser." There was silence on the other side. An uncomfortable silence that didn't sit well with me.

"It's not a good time Kaiser. I'll give you a call tomorrow, okay." I knew her ass was lying and I let her know it.

"Yo ass is lying. I've been blowing your phone up and you've been ducking a nigga. If you back fucking with that homo just say that, Manda. I'm a grown ass man, I can take it." My frustration had reached the top level. We'd been making progress and if she was pushing me to the side so that she could stay with her undercover brother, I wanted her to be up front about it.

I heard the locks on the door turn and I braced myself for what I was gonna see on the other side. The door opened and it felt as if all the air had been sucked out of my body. This was how I should've felt seeing my mother dead at the bakery. The feeling was overwhelming.

"What the fuck happened to your face, Amanda!" I barked. I wanted to stay calm but failed miserably. My future wife stood before with a busted lip, a nasty scratch on her forehead and a black eye. There was gonna be another death in the city today for sure.

"Could you keep your voice down and come inside," she hissed while peeking out into the hallway.

"Why you peeking out here, the motherfucka that did that to

your face just left or something?" Now I was even louder as I started to look around.

"Kaiser, please!" She scolded while pulling me by my shirt. "This is why I said I was gonna call you on the phone. I didn't want you to see me like this and start losing your mind. I handled everything already."

"Aaron bitch ass did that shit to your face didn't he." I bit the inside of my mouth in an effort to keep from punching a hole in her wall. When she didn't answer immediately it told me all I needed to know. "Bet." Taking my phone out of my pocket, I sent a message to one of my hittas. All I did was text Aaron's name. He already knew what the message meant and what to do next.

"I said I took care of it."

"How did you take care of it Amanda if you're standing in front of me with your face all twisted." As soon as the words left my mouth, I wanted to take them back. Shaking her head, she walked away, leaving me standing in her hallway looking stupid. I heard a door slam and wanted to kick my own ass for being so insensitive. Following behind her, I knocked on the only door that was closed.

"Aye, I'm sorry about that, ma," I spoke through the door. That was real whack of me. I'm fucked up seeing you like this and I'm not thinking. If you don't wanna talk about it, that's fine but I'm not leaving either. I'll be right here when you come out." Making myself comfortable in front of the door, I sat down on the floor with my head in my hands. Today had been a hell of a day and it wasn't even twelve o' clock yet.

Now I knew why she was ducking me and it was for good reason. Her bruises looked about a day old. I'm sure had I seen them on the first day, I wouldn't have been able to stick around to console her. This was the reason why I didn't want her coming home. I didn't want to think about how she ended up with the bruises, but I knew that her confronting dude about his secret life wasn't gonna be easy. Hearing the door open, I looked up to see her walk out in a robe.

I couldn't read her so I just stared up at her. I wanted to look away because the bruises on her face had me ready to say fuck putting somebody on and go out to find him myself. I knew I needed to be with her though. She wouldn't admit it out loud but she needed me right now. She needed me two days ago and had she called, I would've been here. Just as I went to say something, she sat down next to me on the floor and rested her head on my shoulder.

"Thank you for coming," she whispered loud enough for me to hear. I placed a kiss on her forehead and put her hand in mine.

"I'ma always come for you, ma. I'm sorry that I didn't get the hint sooner. I know I said you don't have to talk about what happened, I just want you to know that I'm gonna take care of it. I may not be able to erase the memory or the pain but I'll eliminate the source of it."

"I was just about to get in the tub when you came. Do you wanna take a bath with me?" She was deflecting. If her method of healing was to block out what happened, I was gonna roll with it.

"Yea. You got bubbles and shit?" She nodded her head yes while giggling.

"Candles too. It's very relaxing." Seeing her smile through her pain, I admired her strength.

"Aight, come on." I stood and held out my hand to help her up.

"I love you," she blurted out with a blank look on her face.

"Are you testing it out to see how it sounds out loud? If so, it sounded good," I joked, not wanting to read too much into it.

"No, I mean it. Unfortunately it took this traumatic experience to really wrap my head around the feeling but I do love you." Using my hand to lift her chin, I kissed her lips softly.

"It's about damn time. I love you too." She smiled and kissed me again. The chase was over and now she was right where she needed to be. I was gonna make sure that I filled her with so much love that she forgot anyone that was before me. We both knew that there would be none after me.

23

AMANDA

I knew that Kaiser was going to show up at my apartment at
some point, I just thought that by that time I'd be fully
healed. I'd been ignoring his calls and everyone else's in
an attempt to get my mind right. Despite my demeanor, I still
wasn't quite there. Never in a million years would I have thought
that Aaron would pull a bitch ass stunt like this. It threw me for a
loop because I initially didn't go into our conversation thinking
that we'd end up tussling.

*When Kaiser dropped me off in front of my building, he
offered to help me upstairs but I declined in case Aaron was
home. Although he wasn't feeling my reasoning, he knew he had
to respect it. I gave him a quick hug and a kiss on the cheek
before exiting the car. Pulling my luggage into the building, I
took a deep breath before stepping into the elevator. I thought of
all the different ways the conversation could go left and kept
thinking of a way to get to a happy medium. I came up blank.
There was no good way to go about bringing up the topic of him
being gay or bisexual.*

Entering my apartment, I knew that he hadn't made it home

because the place was just as I had left it. I breathed a small sigh of relief because it gave me sometime to pack as much of his belongings as I could before he showed up. Pulling my bags into the room, I put them behind my door. My next stop was to the closet that we shared. His side was filled with a bunch of expensive shit. The bitch in me wanted to spring clean and bleach all his shit but I knew it would do nothing for the situation.

Dragging his MCM luggage from the back of the closet, I began pulling his clothes from the hangers. The more I packed, the more emotional I became. I still couldn't grasp the fact that Aaron had willingly put my life in danger all because he couldn't be real with me or himself. At the end of the day, I felt like what he did with his body was my business, especially when it came to sexual relationships. Tears fell freely down my face, thinking about the time I had wasted second guessing myself during the last year of the relationship.

Closing one bag, I reached for another. I continued the packing assembly until I heard my front door open and close. Jumping up from the foot stool that I sat on, I walked out of the closet, ready for whatever. As I took steps toward the living room, I could hear him talking on the phone. He was using the speaker freely thinking that I wasn't home.

"Yea, babe, I just walked inside," I heard him say.

"Okay. Have you been able to talk to Amanda yet?" The person I assumed was his lover said on the other end.

"No, I didn't," Aaron responded, frustrated. "I already told you that I would when the time was right. You trying to rush me into doing it on your time ain't gon' work."

"You keep thinking that excuse is gonna fly with me is gonna have you without a woman or a man, keep it up."

I wanted to throw up in my mouth hearing that. This motherfucka was really having his way with this shit. Having heard enough, I came around the corner to make my presence known. I watched his eyes grow twice the size and he quickly let his lover know that he would call him back later. He couldn't find the words to say as he set his phone down on the kitchen island, so I spoke first.

"How long have you been attracted to men?"

"I'm not attracted to men." He lied with a straight face.

"See, the lying is gonna piss me the fuck off and make this conversation even more difficult than it already is. At this point, you owe me the decency of the truth Aaron. So let me ask you again, when did you start liking niggas? Is this something new, or was it always your thing and I missed the signs? Are you living out a fantasy? I threw out question after question, becoming more highly annoyed that he was standing there on mute.

"Bitch I ain't fucking gay!" He barked. "I don't know what you talking bout and I don't know where you getting that shit from." He called himself storming out of the kitchen and past me. He had me so fucked up thinking that his outburst was gonna get me off his ass. I was right on his heels.

"So what do you call fucking other men then, Aaron? Is it something you do for fun?" Before I knew what was happening, he had spun around and punched me in my face. "Owwww," I yelled out as the pain seemed to move throughout my whole face. "You motherfucka!" I shrieked and charged at him.

Aaron had me by at least eighty pounds, so I knew I couldn't beat him but that didn't stop me from trying. We tussled all in the hallway, with him trying his best to keep me restrained. I was getting my licks in, making sure to hit him in all of his vulnerable places. Somehow we ended up on the floor and I hit my head on the edge of the wall.

"Fuck, Amanda! Baby, stop fighting, you're bleeding." Hearing him call me baby only made me fight harder. Lifting my leg up, I was able to knee him in the balls. "Arghhh, fuck," he yelled out and rolled off of me.

I jumped up, running off of pure adrenaline. I was in pain from my wounds and I felt something wet coming down the side of my face which I'm sure was blood. My heart hurt more than my wounds though. My pride was fucked up and more than anything, my ego was bruised. Having to walk around knowing that the man I'd given my all to had been secretly sleeping with men was enough to make me wanna kill his ass.

"Get your shit and get the fuck out of my house, Aaron. I wanna forget that I ever met your ass."

"Are you comfortable staying here?" Kaiser asked from behind me as he washed my back.

"Yea, I'll be fine. Why, you tryna move in with me?" I joked.

"Whatever you need me to do to make you feel safe again, I'm with that." He kissed the side of my head, making me smile.

"You being here is making me feel safe. Thank you for not taking no for an answer. You always seem to know when I need you the most."

"You be taking a nigga through changes forreal. You're worth it though, that's for damn sure." I giggled and put my back against his chest.

"What were you doing before you came over?"

"Man, you wouldn't believe me if I told you."

"Try me."

"My mother is dead," he said in a very monotone voice. He was so emotionless that for a moment I didn't believe him. Turning back around, I searched for the truth.

"Don't play like that Kaiser." His facial expression didn't change.

"I'm dead ass. Me and Kaiser found her dead at her bakery today. Shit was crazy."

"Kaiser, are you okay?" I asked, genuinely concerned.

"Yea, are you okay? Why you looking at me like that?"

"Probably because you just told me that your mother died and your reaction is throwing me."

"Oh, I said it was fucked up. That's all I got, ma." He shrugged his shoulders. "Look, I don't want you to think I'm some cold hearted person. I never had a relationship with my mother growing up. That was her choice, not mine. The last time I seen her was brief and that interaction reminded me why me and my brother did our own thing. I'm not gonna act like I'm broken up behind her death. You can't miss what you never had." While I agreed with the statement, my heart still went out to him.

"Whenever you wanna talk about what that was like growing up, you have my ear." We stayed in the tub until the water got cold. For the rest of the day, we lounged around my apartment, doing nothing. Once night fell, I fell into a peaceful slumber in Kaiser's arms. Aaron, nor our altercation crossed my mind not once.

IT HAD BEEN a week since Kaiser had popped up at my house to check in on me. He stayed for two nights straight and I had to nearly push him out the door so that he could tend to his business. He figured that because I still hadn't told him the details of what happened between Aaron and I that I was having a hard time. I assured him that I was good and ready to get back to my day to day after my brief break. It was cute how he doted on me the entire time. He had even spoke to my mother on the phone, making sure to let her know that I was in better hands now. He didn't know it, but she was gonna hold him to those words.

Today, I had plans to meet up with Domonique and Kelly for lunch. It was time to go over the final details of putting my salon together so that I could get the business opened. If my experience with Aaron made anything clear to me, it was that I no longer had time to waste. I hadn't spoken to the girls since we'd been back from Columbia. They'd reached out but like Kaiser's messages and calls, I didn't respond. I was ready to sit down with them and update them on what went down with me and Aaron, who I surprisingly hadn't heard from since I put him out.

Grabbing my keys and purse, I headed towards the door when my phone rang in my hand. Aaron's mothers' name flashed on the screen and I sighed. It was rare that we spoke and if we did it was because Aaron initiated the conversation. Other than that she barely showed much interest in me and the feeling was mutual. I contemplated not answering but thought, what the hell.

"Hello," I spoke into the phone. I could hear what sounded like sniffling on the other end of the line. "Hello, Ms. Jennifer, is everything okay?"

"No, and I don't think it will be. Aaron was shot. He's in the hospital."

"What?!" I screeched. "Shot, when?"

"A week ago. I'm here in the hospital with him now. I'm aware that you two are no longer together but figured you'd want to know. According to the doctors the bullet traveled to his spine and he may not be able to walk again."

"Oh, my god. Thank you for letting me know. I'm so sorry to hear that. Please let him know that he's in my prayers." I paused for a second before speaking again. "Do you think I could—. You know what, nevermind. Just let him know that I wish him a speedy recovery."

"Sure. And I want you to know that I understand how you feel and why you had to leave. While I don't agree with Aaron's lifestyle, I know that I love my son. I also know that you loved my son. Don't think that his choices reflect on you, who you are as a woman, and what you bring to the table. Sometimes the heart just wants what the heart wants." I let her words sink in and concluded that Aaron's secret life was only kept a secret from me. Having heard enough, I said my goodbyes.

"Thank you for that. Knowing that information about his lifestyle would have come in handy years ago but this was a lesson learned. You have a good day, Ms. Jennifer. I hung up the phone and walked out the door. Karma was nothing nice and Aaron was in the beginning stages of finding out. I could thank Kaiser for aiding in me seeing past where I thought my relationship was. I guess I came out on the winning end of things after all.

24

DOMINIQUE

I decided to opt out of lunch with the girls at the last minute. I felt bad because I did miss them and needed to be around some positive vibes. Ever since that fateful day when I became a victim of circumstance, my head has been all fucked up. The truths that were revealed that day still had my mind reeling. I had even taken a step back from Karma. He objected but I felt that it was best to put a little distance between us so that we could both sort out our feelings.

I mean, I killed this man's mother for god sake. Although he expressed that he didn't blame me for what happened and that she was behind the fire at his lounge, the facts are she was still his mother. I was still tryna wrap my head around that. The woman I knew as my mother's best friend and my godmother had a whole family that I knew nothing about. It took a certain amount of, I don't give a fuck to not acknowledge your own children. It took a cold hearted person to plot on them all in the name of greed.

I sent Viv a message letting her know that today would be my only day to meet up with her. I didn't want to give her the option to choose the date or time for us to talk because I didn't want her to think that she was in control. She agreed to meet me at her bakery before it opened and that was fine with me seeing as I was already up. I threw on a cropped hoodie, a pair of jeans, and a pair of sneakers. Grabbing my keys, I made my way out the door.

I probably should've mentioned this meet up to my therapist seeing as it was a step towards addressing the pain from my past. At the last minute, I decided not to in the event that things went left. On the drive to the bakery, I thought about what I wanted to say once I was face to face with Viv. More than anything, I wanted to know why she took on the role of my godmother when she knew she didn't want the responsibility. Pulling into the parking lot, I sent a text letting her know that I had arrived.

She responded back, letting me know that the front door was open and to walk to the back. Getting out of my car, I said a quick prayer before entering the restaurant. Following her directions, I walked to the back.

"In here, Dom," I heard her say. Turning the corner, I found her sitting behind a desk in her office. The way she sat with her hands folded on her desk, and a devious smile on her face irked me. "You can come in and have a seat."

I walked inside of the office and scanned the room. "I'm good with standing."

"It's good to see you after all these years," she said while standing up and walking around the desk. "You're doing pretty well for yourself. I always knew that you'd land on your feet."

"Yea, those survival skills usually kick in when you're discarded like yesterday's trash," I shot back with a petty comment of my own.

"Ahh," she said, "still playing the victim role I see. I wonder how that works with my son."

My face frowned up and I cocked my head to the side. "Excuse me? First off, I've never played the victim. If it's one thing I am, it's resilient. I made shit happen while living in your *house and when I was put out. You were quick to throw me out all while pocketing the money that was left to me. I let you have that because I knew there was bigger and better out there for me. And who is this son you speak of?" As far as I knew she didn't have any children.*

"Karma."

"Girl, Karma who?" I responded, confused.

"How many Karma's do you know that own a club?" As I let her words sink in my hands started to get clammy. The only thing that went off in my head was set up. Had he known my story all along and used my past as a way to get close to me? "Don't beat yourself up trying to figure out the who, what, where, and how's. Karma has no clue that we're family."

"I wouldn't consider us family and I see now why he feels the same way. I spent years under your roof after my mother passed and I've never seen any indication that you had kids."

"You've known me for a while now, there's not a nurturing bone in my body. I don't have the emotional availability to take care of children and I own that whole heartedly. Hence the reason why they stayed with their father. Anyway, let's get to the reason why I reached out. I need you to do me a favor, just like old times."

I chuckled, thinking she must be out of her rabbit ass mind. "Where is Ashton Kutcher because I know for a fact that I'm being punk'd." I looked around waiting for someone to jump out.

"All I need for you to do is get Karma down to this address." She pulled a piece of paper from her pocket and went to hand it to me. I looked at her like she had lost her damn mind but the expression on her face told me that she was very serious. "Tell him that you have information on the people who set fire to his club. I'll take care of the rest."

"I want you to know that I mean this with the utmost disrespect. Hell fucking no. There's a special place in hell for people like you. You already left a void by choosing not to be in their

lives, now you wanna come back in plotting their downfall. You're lucky I don't fight the elderly because I really wanna take it there witchu right about now."

"Unfortunately for you, I don't fight but I do know my way around one of these." She pulled out a small handgun from behind her desk and closed the space between us. Pointing the gun at my forehead, she smirked. "Now, do you wanna use your phone or mine to make that call?"

Tight lipped, I held my composure. Although the gun was small in size, I didn't underestimate the damage the bullet could do. With my hands held out for her to see, I swallowed hard before speaking.

"You didn't have me come here to kill me. I'm gonna reach in my bag to grab my phone."

"Reach slowly. I'd hate to have to put a nice size hole in that pretty face of yours."

"Why are you doing this?"

"It's simple, they owe me," she casually said while shrugging their shoulders. "I put good years into their father and his drug business before he decided that it was time for me to take a step back and give him children. The deal was, I give him the kids, and he would continue to provide me with the lifestyle I was accustomed to while he took care of them. He reneged on that deal and now I want what's rightfully mine. Koran is dead and gone and I know he left money to his precious sons. They gotta cut me in or get cut out."

"You are a piece of work and I hope that Karma forgives me for this." Catching her off guard, I raised my phone and hit her in the face with it.

"Ouch," she yelled out, stumbling back. It gave me a chance to smack the gun out of her hand. Before she had a chance to recover I was on her ass like white on rice.

I sent hits to her body for me and her kids. She got some hits in but they were no match for the blows that I was throwing.

Somehow we ended up tripping over a chair and falling over. Seeing the gun in my sights, we both went to reach for it at the same time. I was in a tussle for my life. We struggled for a few minutes before the gun went off. Pop!

I froze up and felt like my heart had gave out. Neither one of us moved but I heard a groan come from Viv. Coming to the conclusion that I hadn't been shot after feeling no pain, I pushed her off of me. She rolled over and when I looked down at her there was no life in her eyes. It was then that I realized she was the one shot. Quickly jumping into action, I grabbed the gun and started for the door to leave out only to run right into Kaiser and Karma.

I hadn't been able to sleep much since then. I was too afraid that the police would come knocking at my door. Karma assured me that he had everything taken care of but it would never be taken care of as long as the incident was still etched in my mind. My phone vibrated on the bed next to me and I reached for it. Seeing a group message from Kelly and Amanda, I opened it up.

TheGirls: Heyy, we miss you. We're gonna give you another day or so to yourself before we pop up. Love you, call us if you need anything.

Me: Aww, I miss y'all too and thank you.

I wanted to tell them what was going on with me but I didn't know when I'd ever be comfortable sharing that news. Setting my phone down, I threw my head back on the bed. My doorbell rang and I chuckled, thinking that the girls had changed their minds about giving me that day or two. Getting up, I walked over to the door.

"I hope y'all brought some food with y'all," I said out loud. Looking through the peephole, I froze when I stared straight into the peephole. Unlocking the door, I held it open while leaning up against it. "What are you doing here?"

"I think I've had enough space from you to last awhile. Can I come in?"

"Yea, sure." I stepped aside, allowing him to come in.

"How you feeling?" He asked.

"Honestly, I've been better. How have you been?"

"Busy. Working around the clock trying to get the lounge back up and running. I wanted to come by and let you know face to face that everything has been taken care of. You can start getting back to some form of normalcy now. I know it won't be an easy thing to forget about, but I want you to know that you're good."

"How do you do it?" I asked him.

"Do what?"

"Act like nothing happened?"

"The same way she acted as if me and Kaiser never existed, is the same way I feel about her. I'm not one to live in the past. I can only pray for her soul at this point. My concern right now is you and where we stand."

"I feel like this is gonna be a stumbling block for us. I mean here we are in the getting to know you stage and then this. This is big Karma. It ain't like I stole your car or something, I killed your mother."

"So what do you propose?"

"More time." He dropped his head and sighed.

"Aight." He grabbed me by my hand and pulled me to him. "I can give you that as long as you give me your word that you're not gonna start building the wall back up with the blocks I just knocked down."

"I promise." We kissed to seal the promise and he let me go. I knew that what I was doing was for the best even if he couldn't admit it. Revisiting my past had threw me for a loop and I didn't want to take him on the rollercoaster ride with me. Karma deserved the fullness of me and once my mental was back, he'd have just that.

Amanda

"Welcome to the Re grand opening of Karma's lounge. I wanna thank y'all for coming out to fuck with me tonight and being patient during this whole process. Sorry y'all had patronize those other establishments with they watered ass drinks." The crowd erupted with laughs as Karma spoke. "Nah, forreal though, we back and better than ever baby. Everybody take a shot on me tonight. DJ, play that shit."

The DJ dropped Meek Mill *Dreams and Nightmares* as Karma exited the stage and walked right into Domonique's arms. I watched from the V.I.P booth as they embraced each other and smiled. It was good to see her back in good spirits. I still didn't know what happened that she had to take a hiatus from the group and I thought it best not to ask. It felt good to be in good spirits and around good vibes after all that had gone down a couple months back.

"Ay, hold up wait a minute, y'all thought I was finished. When I bought that Aston Martin y'all thought I was finished.

Ayeee," Kelly danced her way over to me with two drinks in her hand.

"Oh, you turning up tonight. You must've gotten that nanny after all," I said while laughing and taking one of the drinks from her.

"Nope, my mother." She stuck her tongue out and threw her hands in the air. Tonight wasn't only a celebration for the re-grand opening of Karma's but it was also a pre celebration for the grand opening of my salon tomorrow night. After all of my hard work, it was finally my time to shine. The journey was a long one but I wouldn't change one moment because I knew the reward was going to be worth it.

"This place is packed out. Why I almost had to knock a bitch down just to get over here to y'all. We can't be down here in the lil' V.I.P with all the common folks. Let's go upstairs to the skybox," Domonique said to us. I bust out laughing.

"You think we can get into the skybox? I heard the owner is very particular about who he lets up there," I said, jokingly.

"I mean, I think we can manage once I give the owner a little something to convince him to let us up there," she blushed while winking.

"And scene," Kelly shouted, "let's go before Micah comes down here looking for me." We all laughed and moved through the crowd.

Making our way up to the skybox, we were let up by security. This was a feature that I was happy that Karma had kept. I liked that it was exclusive and made for his people only. Entering the room, I made a beeline right for Kaiser, who was standing at the window. Setting my drink down, I wrapped my arms around his neck.

"Were you watching me the whole time I was down there?"

"You damn right. You in here witcha thighs out and shit, I'ma be at this window every time." I laughed, knowing that he was serious.

"You are something else."

"Yea, so they say." I pecked his lips and he wrapped his hands around my waist. "You know this could've been us a long time ago right."

"Oh, yea?"

"Yep. I could've been wining and dining you and showing you things." He smiled and I couldn't help but smile back.

"You know good things come to those who wait right."

"And even greater things come to those who wait even longer."

I chuckled and rested my head on his chest. This security that I found in Kaiser was unmatched. He was everything that I never knew I needed, and I now knew, who to run to......